When Life Tumbles In

A Story of Hope for All Who Face Loss

Kenneth E. Field

REVIEW AND HERALD® PUBLISHING ASSOCIATION
HAGERSTOWN, MD 21740

Copyright © 2003 by
Review and Herald® Publishing Association
All rights reserved

The author assumes full responsibility for the accuracy of all facts and quotations as cited in this book.

This book was
Edited by Gerald Wheeler
Designed by Tina Ivany
Cover art by Stone/Michael Orton/Getty Images
Electronic makeup by Shirley M. Bolivar
Typeset: Veljovic Book 11/14

PRINTED IN U.S.A.
07 06 05 04 03   5 4 3 2 1

R&H Cataloging Service
Field, Kenneth Eugene, 1954-
   When life tumbles in: a story of hope for those who face loss.

   1. Title.

813.52

ISBN 0-8280-1724-7

Also by Kenneth Field:
   Second Rescue

   To order, call 1-800-765-6955
   Visit us at www.reviewandherald.com for information on other Review and Herald® products.

Dedication

For Carol, my wife,
the love of my life, who came
very close to dying, and didn't.

For the Iliffs—
Lloyd, Noreen, Michael, Michelle,
Heather, and Jeffrey, who never quit.

For my parents, Ralph and Hazel,
who were better parents than I ever realized.

For my brother Rick and his family,
whose lives seem charmed only because they make
hard work look easy.

Contents

1	The Day the World Ended	11
2	Waiting on God	16
3	Sleeping Beauty	24
4	Putting Away Childish Things	28
5	A Long, Long Row to Hoe	34
6	Who Your Friends Are	38
7	Holding On	43
8	No Place Like Home	47
9	Blue Christmas	57
10	Resolution	62
11	Running Away	67
12	Dark of Night	71
13	Breaking Point	77
14	Thin Ice	86
15	Changing Directions	91
16	Where To From Here?	95
17	Knowing When to Run	99
18	Surprises	103
19	The Whole Truth, and Nothing But	108
20	On the Road to Damascus	111
21	One Foot in Front of the Other	115
22	The Wall	124
23	Down Time	127

Acknowledgments

No book is ever written in complete isolation. A number of very important people assisted with the birthing of this one, and I'd like to give them credit.

First, to my wife, Carol, who not only set this story in motion as a result of an unfortunate and nearly tragic accident, but who supplied me with information about occupational therapy. This time I paid attention.

Second, to Deputy Sheriff Darrell "Spider" Spidell, who graciously helped me to represent a law officer properly. I wanted it right, and Spider helped me get there.

To Cynthia Prevoski, Robin Collins, and Cheri Gustafson, who read various drafts and gave me considerable feedback when I sorely needed it.

And last, though certainly not least, to the men and women of the editorial staff of the Review and Herald® Publishing Association, who did the nuts-and-bolts stuff that editors do to make a story into a book. In particular, I'd like to mention Jeannette Johnson, acquisitions editor, who walked me through it step by step; and to Richard Coffen, assistant to the president, who believed in me enough two decades ago to give me a chance. Thanks to all of you!

Foreword

Bad things happen. It seems a fact of life that we all encounter a share of pain and suffering. We look around and ask, "Why us? What did we do to deserve this? Is there something wrong with us?" As common as these questions are, as certain as they will be asked, they are the wrong questions, and the answers, if indeed any are found, make little sense at all to our limited points of view. Simple cause and effect doesn't always work in the realm of human experience. But if we look to God for guidance, to others for companionship, and to within our hearts for our true beliefs, we may discover how to transcend our personal sorrows and by the grace of God, truly live.

"When I was a child, I spake as a child, I understood as a child, I thought as a child: but when I became a man, I put away childish things. For now we see through a glass, darkly; but then face to face: now I know in part; but then shall I know even as also I am known" (1 Cor. 13:11, 12).

1

The Day the World Ended

It was raining, and Doug didn't see the car.

He could just about hear Gramma's voice in his head as he pedaled through the downpour the Huffy bicycle he'd bought on special at Kmart down Atkinson Street.

That boy isn't smart enough to come in out of the rain!

Unfortunately, though, he had to admit, grimacing into the spatter of rain dripping off his helmet, in this case at least she was absolutely right.

The women of his family had all the good sayings. His mother was from Kansas, and her favorite comment was that someone "didn't have sense enough to pound sand in a rat hole." Or his sister's observation about people being "one plate short of a picnic." At various times in his life Doug had been guilty of all three descriptions. This was just one more time.

The rain had begun a half hour into his ride, too far from home to make much difference in how wet he got. What didn't soak him pouring down from the sky got him splashing off the knobby tires of the mountain bike. Without fenders on the bike, he had no protection from the groundwater sluicing up his back, spraying out in a fine pinwheel, wet and cold. Traffic had eased a bit, but the hiss of passing cars all but deafened him. At first he'd ridden with extra caution, his head swiveling back and forth, tracking on cars and drivers that might be threats. But as the rain wore on—as he got colder and his fingers stiffer despite the wool gloves—he grew gradually less vigilant, finally just pedaling for home, head down, suffering.

Doug was looking forward now to warm, dry towels, fresh clothing, delicious heat, and the cessation of the pain in the muscles just above his knees. It was the only part of his body that seemed not to feel the cold or the rain. He lived for the fantasy of

When Life Tumbles In

hanging the bike from its hooks in the garage, of stumbling weak-kneed into the house and directly into a shower so hot it would peal the skin right off his back. Breathing in warm mist that would open his lungs like clenched fists releasing their grip.

Coming up on Thornton, he would take a quick right and see home two blocks down. Standing on the pedals, he tried to shake out the leg muscles.

It saved his life.

A car brushed past him, so close that he could have leaned against its side if he'd chosen, a silver T-Bird that went by in a cloud of cold water and took the same sharp right onto Thornton that he'd planned. Throwing all his weight back over the rear tire, he slammed on both hand brakes, fully expecting to go down. The car missed his front tire by inches. Somehow he didn't fall. But as the car accelerated quickly away from the corner, Doug stood trembling, too shattered even to shout or to shake his fist. Whoever it was hadn't even seen him, didn't know how close to disaster they'd both come.

His teeth began to chatter, and the fantasy of warmth vanished. All he wanted now was to make it home alive. And, he decided, he would walk his bike the last couple blocks just to make sure that happened.

His bike left hanging, dripping, from its hooks in the garage behind him, Doug trudged up the stepping-stones, across the backyard, and onto the back porch. His hands fumbled with the doorknob, but the dry warmth of the laundry room was like a gentle ocean wave on the skin of his face. He popped open the dryer door and snatched out a still-warm towel. Scrubbing his face, he breathed in the warmth, and muscles all over his body began to relax.

Kicking off his drenched tennis shoes, he then peeled off the socks. He would come back down later, wring them out, and toss them into the wash, but he couldn't face it just now. Doug climbed the back stairs, dragging himself up by the railing, his leg muscles

The Day the World Ended

complaining. After stripping off his wet clothing, he tossed it into the hamper and headed for the shower he'd promised himself. Then he shoved aside his sister's "foo foo" cleansers, turned the spray up hard and hot, and let the water pour down on his head. It took several minutes before his hands would open and close normally, and almost at the same time, the memory of the near accident came back to him in a rush of adrenaline.

The blur of a rainslicked car brushing past him in a wash of silver spray, his heart in his throat.

Beginning to shake again, he steadied himself with a hand against the shower wall. It was time to get out of the shower.

Toweled dry and dressed in blue jeans and a green flannel work shirt, he came back downstairs with his wet things and started another load of laundry. The phone rang while he was adding soap, but his mother answered it in the front room. The washing machine started up and drowned out the conversation. He slipped his wet tennis shoes next to the baseboard heater and padded out to the front room in his stockinged feet.

His mother was just hanging up.

"Who was that?" he asked.

He'd been expecting a call from his girlfriend, Jill. They were both headed off to college in the fall, and the anticipation was getting to them. The two of them had begun going over the lists of classes offered in the latest college bulletin, planning, discussing, and revising plans. Doug hoped that all the energy they'd expended making plans would simplify registration once they actually stepped on campus. Besides, doing anything with Jill was worth the time.

Only after repeating the question did he notice how stiffly his mother stood, fragile as fine crystal, her hand still on the phone in its cradle.

"Mom?"

She still hadn't said anything, and a sudden chill, not

entirely caused by the rain, set him to shivering. His mother turned slowly, her eyes downcast, the lines in her face deeper than he'd remembered.

"That was your father . . . at the hospital. Catherine's been hurt."

When she looked up at him, her eyes were dark. She bit her lip, and her hands began to flutter, until she noticed them and forced them to her side.

"You'd better drive," she said quietly. Doug picked up the keys from the table in the entry hall and stepped into a dry pair of sneakers sitting on a mat beside the front door. Suddenly he didn't feel a thing. No surge of fear, no flush of concern. Nothing. For a moment he wondered why. He saw everything with unnatural clarity. But while his awareness had become extra sensitive, his emotions—his "feelings"—seemed absent.

The family car—a decade-old green Mercury, its surface beaded with rainwater—sat in the driveway. Doug saw every dent and scratch as he came down the walk. He'd learned to drive in this car, borrowed it for dates, and now he would use it to get to Cat as fast as he could. Sliding into the driver's seat, he turned the key, and it started immediately, a familiar rumbling under the hood. After leaning across the seat and pushing the passenger door open for his mother, he then buckled his own seat belt.

His senses seemed to be alert to things he normally screened out. He saw the stoplight at the intersection on Atkinson cycle as he backed out of the driveway, noticing another car getting a slight jump on the light. Its license plate indicated it must be from out of state, and he wondered if the driver was enjoying his visit.

Doug's mind skipped from here to there, examining his world under a kind of brilliant light turned on, it seemed, just for him. He felt the texture of the road through his hands on the steering wheel, heard the tires whisk over wet pavement—all as if he'd never driven in the rain before.

"What did Dad say?" he asked his mother as she sat stiffly next to him, her purse clutched in her lap. "What happened to Cat?"

"I don't know much," she answered.

The Day the World Ended

Doug saw her take in breath, ragged and shallow. She did not seem to notice the tears spilling from her eyes. With an icy calm he realized that his mother was on the edge of panic. But it was just another bit of information, another fragment of the stream of data.

"Where did she go after breakfast?" he prompted.

"Brian came by," she said, on firmer ground now. "They were going to the mall to meet friends."

Brian. Not one of Doug's favorite people. The boy was athletic, smart, handsome, and Cat's dearest friend. But Doug saw him as self-involved, brashly overconfident, and reckless. The two of them had not had words. Doug was starting college in the fall while Brian was, like Cat, only a sophomore at Sehome High School, but the feelings were mutual. They avoided each other whenever possible.

"When did they leave?"

"Just after you went out on your bike. Catherine said she'd be back by dinner. Then your father called from the hospital, saying that she'd been in a car accident. The hospital had contacted him. I guess they found his phone number in her purse. They wanted . . . needed his . . ."—she began to waver—"permission . . . to operate," she forced out.

"On what?"

"Your father didn't say. Just that it was serious and time was important, so he gave permission."

"Was Brian driving that old clunker?"

"It's paid for," she said, as she always had whenever he disparaged Brian's car.

"That car is older than I am," Doug pointed out, not for the first time. "No airbags . . ."

"Can we change the subject, please?" his mother said in that tone that meant the subject was changed whether he liked it or not.

"Sure, Mom," he agreed, pulling into the hospital parking lot and easing into a space as close to the emergency ward as possible.

He didn't want to worry his mother unnecessarily, but he knew Brian a lot better than she did. One of the things he was aware about the boy was that trouble found him irresistible.

2

Waiting on God

The hospital was another world entirely. Although he couldn't remember ever being in the ER before, it made Doug uneasy. It was new, unfamiliar territory, certainly, but that wasn't the reason for his distress. Not did it explain why his hands were sweating. Maybe it was the fluorescent lights with their buzzing undertone, perhaps the presence of hospital personnel in their whites and greens, or it could even be the smell of antiseptic. He knew that one got used to unusual things after time, but Doug wanted to hold the whole experience at arm's length.

If he allowed himself to drop his barrier of artificial calm, Doug would have to admit that Cat was here, that she was really hurt, and that all the people he cared about in the whole world stood teetering on the brink. His life and those of his family were changing—right here, right now. No going back, no crossed fingers.

Carter Walker, Doug's father, stood with his back to the entrance to the ER, speaking with a uniformed deputy sheriff. He didn't see them come in.

"Carter?" Doug's mother called, her voice quavering. "Where's Catherine?"

Doug's father was a tall, spare man, hair going to gray. Since he still had his name badge clipped to the pocket of his dress shirt, his tie carefully knotted at his throat, he must have come straight from the store.

"Nance," was all his father said before hugging his wife fiercely, her arms going round him in reflex.

"What's wrong? Is she . . ."

"No, honey, she's still fighting. It's just . . . she's hurt pretty bad."

"What happened? They were just going to the mall. Was it alcohol? A drunk driver?"

"No, ma'am," the deputy spoke up for the first time, shaking his head. "Single-car accident. No evidence of alcohol at the scene."

The deputy—"Richards," according to the name tag beneath his star—was a big man. He spoke calmly and quietly, his face a careful mask that never really changed. His coat, unzipped and hanging open, was still damp from the rain. The revolver on his hip seemed huge to Doug, but not compared with the man wearing it.

"Deputy Richards," his father said, "this is my wife, Nancy, and my son, Doug."

The deputy nodded politely, the lines in his face softening as he spoke to Doug's mother. His was the face of a man who'd seen more than he was comfortable with. And he'd seen Cat.

"He was just explaining what happened," Mr. Carter said.

The deputy pulled a small notebook out of his breast pocket and glanced down at something he'd written there.

"We got the call about an hour ago," he began. "We had paramedics and a fire team on site with us in under five minutes of the alert."

"Where did it happen?" Father asked.

"Out on the Hannegan, just past the Medcalf Road."

The Hannegan was a long stretch of road that meandered haphazardly along the borders of farm fields lined by six-foot ditches, barbed-wire fencing, and power poles spaced evenly down its entire length. Doug had been through there. *But why out there?* he wondered. Mom had said they were headed to the mall, but the Hannegan was in the opposite direction.

"The information we have on the accident is still sketchy. Folks in another car observed the wreck and called 911 on their cell phone. Really helped our response time.

"Apparently, the car with your daughter and the young man, . . ."—he flipped a page on his notebook—". . . Brian Montgomery, drifted across the center line, then made a sudden sharp correction."

Doug, cursed with an extremely vivid imagination, could see it all in his head: the road slick with rain, the car swerving back into its own lane, the urgent sound of wet tires trying to maintain their grip on the asphalt.

When Life Tumbles In

"The driver may have overcorrected. We won't know for sure until he can tell us. At the scene he was too dazed to be very helpful. The witnesses say the car went onto the shoulder, tried to pull back, and lost the rear end in the ditch. It rolled up on its side . . . the passenger side . . . and struck a phone pole right where the firewall meets the windshield."

In his mind Doug heard tires howling on pavement, the engine revving wildly, the sound of metal crunching, and the solid punch of a wooden phone pole fracturing glass. Then silence.

"We found the driver hanging in his seat belt, partly conscious with an obvious head injury. Your daughter was pinned under the dashboard. She wasn't belted in."

"Oh, no!" his mother breathed, her hand covering her mouth.

"She knows better than that," Mr. Carter chimed in. "She's very careful about that."

"Something we need to ask later when she regains consciousness." Deputy Richards scribbled a note in his pad. "The firefighters had to use the Jaws of Life. They took the car apart, got them both on backboards and stable, then transported them here. Your daughter was never conscious at any time.

"We don't know why your daughter wasn't using her seat belt. Nor do we know why they lost control in the first place. The driver has a prior record for speeding and an illegal turn, but skid marks at the scene didn't indicate excessive speed. A preliminary check of the car shows brakes, tires, and steering in good condition. And as I said before, there was no indication of alcohol. Naturally, the driver's blood will be tested for confirmation."

The deputy paused. Father hugged Mother. Doug listened silently, afraid to move and not knowing why.

"There's just a lot of stuff we won't know until your daughter gets well enough to tell us. My guess is that it was just one of those things. Two kids in the wrong place at the wrong time."

"Thank you. We appreciate how you helped our little girl."

"Just doing the job, Mr. Walker," Deputy Richards replied, before turning to Doug's mother. "I've seen worse, ma'am. Your daughter's alive. I'll think good thoughts for her."

Waiting on God

The deputy shook hands with Doug's father, turned, and walked to the door. He placed his hat on his head before going out into the rain, drops beading up immediately on the plastic slicker protecting his Stetson.

A matronly Black woman, reading glasses perched on her nose, called their name from behind the receptionist's desk.

"Mr. and Mrs. Walker? Could I get some information for the paperwork?"

"Yes, of course," Father said, his voice gone as pale as Mother's face.

Doug turned his back and stuck his hands in his pockets, fists clenched. The mental alertness he'd experienced during the drive to the hospital was now seeping away. Everything around him began to blur. He tried to slow things down by taking inventory of the ER waiting room.

It was deceptively calm here. A couple sat in the back of the room, the woman, stiff with pain, holding a folded cloth against her right eye. The man beside her looked helpless. A young mother sat near the television, watching cartoons with her baby boy, a vacant look in her eyes. Behind Doug, his parents continued to supply information to the receptionist, nodding and speaking in subdued tones. Doug wondered if his own facial expression was as desperate as those around him.

The rain that had fallen almost steadily since his near accident on the bike continued tapping away on the skylights above him, invisible in the failing outdoor light. The rain was not relaxing—he doubted that it ever would be again. Just one more incessant stream of sensory information drowning him. He jingled the change in his pocket and read a framed list of patients' rights on the wall that began, "If you have a medical emergency . . ."

Cat was hurt somewhere inside this place. Doug didn't know what had happened, how badly she'd been injured, or what was being done for her and by whom. He didn't even know where she was in the maze of hospital corridors all tastefully decorated in pastels. And nobody was in any great hurry to tell him either. He was only the brother, after all.

That's what Cat had said to him once.

"You're just the brother," she'd teased him.

It had been the occasion of the high school play. Cat had the lead, playing Emily in Thornton Wilder's *Our Town*. Doug had wanted to come backstage to watch, but the faculty advisor in charge wouldn't allow it. His sister had pointed out that despite his elevated status as a graduating senior, he wasn't part of the production team. Nor was he important enough to rate a backstage pass. He was just the brother of the star.

The play was wonderful anyway. Cat had received a standing ovation, and she'd earned every bit of the applause. Then Doug remembered that her character died in the play. Suddenly he felt very cold.

Brian's parents burst through the emergency room entry. Both of them worked, and the police had apparently had trouble contacting them. A man of average build with a larger than average midriff, Mr. Montgomery went immediately to the reception desk after steering his wife toward them.

"Is there any news?" the woman asked, wringing her hands.

"Not since we got here," Doug's father answered. "Cat is in surgery. We don't know anything about Brian beyond what the police told us."

Mr. Montgomery joined them a second later, saying that he'd asked the receptionist to call someone to talk to them. He didn't hold out much hope that that would happen anytime soon.

"And we have some papers to fill out," he added with a shrug. "I don't know all of the information." Taking his wife's arm, he said, "I need your help." After a couple steps, he stopped, turned and looked sheepish. "I hope Cat's going to be OK," he muttered.

"Thank you," Doug's father said.

Doug had nothing to add to that.

His parents returned to their seats in the waiting room. After completing the paperwork for their son, the Montgomerys joined

Waiting on God

them. Doug's father repeated Officer Richards' report without embellishment, but couldn't answer most of their questions. Having heard the phrase "we don't know" so often, even Doug was getting frustrated. After that, there was nothing to do but wait.

His mother and father maintained an outwardly quiet calm, an almost physical paralysis that hid the frightening rush of thought behind faces closed to emotion. Brian's parents, however, were pacers, going back and forth across the waiting room. Mrs. Montgomery sat briefly from time to time, riffling through a magazine without reading it, then getting up to get a drink from the water fountain. Mr. Montgomery never sat down, tracing a slow, agonized circuit out of the waiting room to stare at the blank doors of the ER, then past the receptionist and the espresso stand to the entry doors to watch the rain, and finally back again to the waiting room. Doug had about reached the point where he was ready to take a baseball bat to the man when a doctor in green scrubs came through the ER doors and looked about.

"Mr. and Mrs. Montgomery?" he asked.

Brian's parents went dead still, then converged on the man.

"How is Brian? Can we see him?" they asked in unison.

"Brian's a lucky young man," the doctor said. "He has a concussion and some minor scrapes and bruises. His head hit something, possibly the visor, and we had to put a few stitches in his forehead. The scarring should be minimal. His memory of the accident is still very hazy, but that may clear in time."

"Can he come home now?" Mrs. Montgomery wanted to know.

"Frankly, I'd like to keep him overnight for observation. Make sure there're no surprises from the head injury."

"Can we see him?" Brian's father asked.

"Certainly. He'll be coming out of ER just down the hall there," the doctor pointed off to one side of the lounge, "and we'll move him up to second floor."

As the Montgomerys hurried off, the doctor turned and extended his hand to Doug's father, a polite nod to his mother.

"You must be the Walkers," he smiled. "I'm Dr. Correia, the attending physician in the ER. I was there when your daughter was

When Life Tumbles In

brought in. I'm sorry I didn't get out to you sooner, but this is the first chance I've had."

Doug's parents stood together, holding each other up. He stayed in his seat, but began to pray silently.

"Dear God . . . ," he whispered.

"Your daughter's injuries are quite serious," Dr. Correia began, speaking softly but firmly. "She was brought into the ER with critical blood loss and trauma to the spinal and cranial regions. Our job was to stabilize her injuries and get her into surgery as quickly as possible. We were fortunate that the response time was so quick and that one of our best surgeons was immediately available."

". . . Cat's hurt bad . . . ," Doug continued.

"We have a number of concerns," the doctor went on. "The blood loss was severe enough to require transfusion. Normally, we like the patient to recover slowly on her own, the situation being what it is with the supply of blood these days. We couldn't afford that in this case."

". . . real bad, God . . ."

"She experienced trauma to her spine and skull as well. The X-rays show varying damage along the spine and some swelling in the cranium. She hasn't regained consciousness since the accident, which is worrisome, but not unusual in this kind of injury. It may have been helpful in one regard, that she didn't move about with a spinal injury."

". . . please, anything You want . . . ," Doug begged in silence.

"I want you to understand," Dr. Correia explained, "that any surgery of this kind is hazardous. She's young and fit—she's got that going for her. But even with complete success, she's not going to come out good as new."

". . . don't let her die, God." Doug's vision blurred as tears flooded his eyes, spilling down his cheeks. *"I'll do anything. I'll give up everything. Whatever You say. Just don't let her die."*

"You should begin preparing yourselves for a major change in your daughter's life," the man said. "She'll need extensive therapy, certainly."

"You mean," Doug's mother asked, "she might be permanently injured?"

The doctor frowned, then went on. "That is a real possibility, though we won't know how seriously for some time. She may be able to recover some or most of her abilities, but probably not all. Even so, with appropriate care she will be able to lead a useful, fulfilling life, but she's going to need help, especially from all of you."

This time the doctor looked at Doug, saw the pain in his eyes, and did not look away. Doug nodded. If Cat needed him, he'd be there. No matter what.

3
Sleeping Beauty

Doug had a picture of Cat in his wallet, her sophomore class picture. She was tall and lean, not thin, with too much muscle to be fashionable. Her face had color, framed by long, sand-blond hair tied back severely in a ponytail, with eyes so light blue she looked blind. That face betrayed her every thought. When she blushed, Father joked that the temperature in the air around her went up five degrees.

This particular class picture was not the first she'd ever given him. That had been one for first grade. He'd been in third grade, and all third-grade boys knew what to do with pictures of first-grade girls, especially if they were their own sisters. When he drew a mustache and a goatee on his sister's smiling face, it had earned him a spanking.

They had fought all through elementary school and into high school, Doug remembered. Typical brother-sister stuff, and both of them gave as good as they got. That was where their nicknames had come from. Since they fought like cats and dogs, Catherine became "Cat," and Doug became "Dog." The only person who absolutely refused to acknowledge the nicknames even existed was their mother. She never used less than their full first names. In fact, Doug could always tell if he was really in trouble when his mother used his middle name, Ralph, too.

The "cat and dog" thing got them in trouble at school as well. On one occasion, when Cat was a brand-new freshman and he a junior, a senior on the track team had interrupted one of their loud "discussions" at their lockers. Being placed side by side because of the alphabetic arrangement decreed by school administrators virtually guaranteed considerable friction. The senior had made a lewd comment, which so astonished Cat that she had no ready comeback. The boy apparently had not realized Doug was her brother, a point he then underscored by blacking the senior's eye. He had to be pulled off the boy by two other students and the vice principal doing hall duty.

After serving his allotted detention and suspension, Doug had heard through the grapevine that the senior wanted to meet him "out back" of the school grounds to "finish their discussion." Scared nearly green, Doug went. The other boy hadn't shown, and Doug never learned why. But the word in the halls was that he had shown up, thus assuring his reputation. Later he told Cat that if you wanted to live life, first you had to show up, a lesson he never forgot.

And here he was in a hospital room at the end of a long line of hospital rooms, thinking about his sister's sophomore class picture. Comparing it with the battered, bandaged form lying asleep in the bed in the center of the room.

Asleep for sure, the nurse assured him so. She slept a lot, Cat did. The painkillers did that. Kept you floating—the nurse said—while the body reknit itself. Healed. Or not.

Cat had been awake off and on during the past few days. She'd talked with them. No one had told her much, except that she was hurt, which she'd guessed, but not how badly. His sister had been unable to recall the accident, or even most of that last day. Nobody pressed her to remember. Some things just weren't worth it.

"Hey, you," Cat croaked.

Doug touched her hand, noticed her fingers barely moved.

"Sleeping Beauty," he grinned, his eyes suddenly swimming.

They had that movie on video. But Cat did not look like Sleeping Beauty. She made a noise deep inside her throat that might have been a laugh . . . or a cough. Doug picked up a plastic cup of water with a straw and held it so she could drink.

"Thanks," she said, her voice clearer, though weak. "Mom and Dad?"

"Getting something to eat," he answered. "I wasn't hungry."

Cat made that sound again, only this time Doug was sure it was a laugh.

"So . . . how bad?"

When Life Tumbles In

He knew exactly what she was asking, what she wanted to know, but he wasn't sure how to answer her.

"I'm probably the wrong person to ask," he finally decided on.

"Still asking," she replied.

"You were hurt pretty bad in the accident," he said, hoping she would let him stay as vague as possible.

"I remember some of that. Not much. But a little."

"Your spine was damaged. That's what they're most concerned about."

"My spine?" Cat closed her eyes. "Am I going to walk out of here?"

He didn't know what to say, conscious that his delay in responding was itself telling her something as well.

"Not right away," he finally answered. "What do you remember about the accident?" he asked, changing the subject.

Cat blinked and cleared her throat. "We were going to the mall. Brian and me."

"Yes," Doug nodded.

"We were going to pick up Brian's cousin Teri. She lives out on the Hannegan."

"That explains why you were out there. Anything else?"

"Real hazy."

"The doctor said you would be."

"It was a car accident?"

"Uh-huh."

"Brian's car?"

"Yes."

"Is Brian all right?" Cat asked, a queer note in her voice.

"Oh, yes. Brian's just fine," Doug replied, standing and walking to the window. "Little bump on the head, a few stitches, some minor cuts and bruises. Just fine," he gritted his teeth.

He could feel Cat looking at him.

"You're angry."

"Yes."

He knew that she didn't need this kind of stress. Not on top of everything else. But he was helpless before the rush of heat that swept up through him. In fact, he enjoyed it.

It had been three days since the accident. Two days since Brian had been discharged from this very hospital. Not one word from him or his parents. Not a phone call, no flowers, not even a get-well card. Nothing. Doug wanted to discuss his inattention with the little twerp personally . . . in close proximity.

"You're angry at Brian," Cat said in a near mumble.

"He was the driver. He was responsible. And here you are. Where's he?"

There was a quiet knock on the door, it opened slightly, and Brian peered in.

"You decent?" he asked from the door, a quick glance taking in Doug at the window.

"Always," Cat replied, her lips slowly forming a smile. "Come in, Bri."

Her brother said nothing, unclenching his hands by force of will. Brian nodded at him, and he nodded back. The younger man had a square of gauze taped carefully just left of center on his forehead, and he walked very stiffly.

"How are you?" Brian asked Cat as he slid into the chair beside her bed, the one Doug had just vacated. Before she could answer, Doug stepped away from the window, forced his voice to remain calm.

"Hey, Cat. I'm getting hungry. I'm going to check out the cafeteria."

"Thanks, Dog," she said, the relief in her voice obvious to *him* at least. "Bring me back some pizza."

"Yeah, sure. Eat all your Jell-O first."

"Talk later," she promised him.

"You bet. Plenty of time," Doug agreed. He turned to Brian. "Don't tire her out," he said pointedly.

"OK," Brian nodded, his eyes never leaving Cat's face.

Easing the door to the room closed behind him, Doug took a deep breath and let it out with a sigh. Then he walked off down the long line of hospital rooms.

4

Putting Away Childish Things

He found his parents in the hospital cafeteria, eating silently at a table out by the big windows. Now that the sun was shining, the view of the bay from those windows was magnificent. But they weren't looking at the view, each other, or even their food. Dad had a bowl of watery vegetable soup he was sipping without tasting, and Mom was pushing mashed potatoes and desiccated mixed vegetables around on her plate.

Doug had a giant chocolate-chip cookie and a can of soda he'd gotten from the espresso stand at the hospital entrance. He fully expected his mother to lecture him on his choices. She didn't like it when he ate junk, but nothing looked good to him. Sitting at the table with his parents, he watched the cafeteria employees in their hairnets drift back and forth from the counter to the kitchen.

His mother didn't seem to notice what he was eating, even when he popped the pull tab on his soda. She did, however, push aside her own food.

"I should get back to Catherine," she said, shoving her chair back.

"Brian Montgomery's visiting her," Doug commented.

"Oh." But she didn't scoot the chair back to the table. "I expect they have some things to say to each other. I'll wait a bit before going up."

"You need to eat something, Nance," her husband said.

She forked a lima bean, put it in her mouth, and chewed. "Nothing tastes good."

Doug broke off a silver dollar-sized bit of his cookie and offered it to her. She smiled, the first time he'd seen her do that in days, and took it.

"Thank you, Douglas." She nibbled delicately at what would have been a single bite for him.

Putting Away Childish Things

"I got in touch with the insurance company," Dad said to no one in particular.

Carter Walker often thought out loud when he was trying to get his mind around something. He'd been doing it more often lately.

"What did they say?" Mom asked.

"The usual song and dance. How sorry they were about the accident, and how they hoped Cat would recover quickly. I gave them all the information. They said they'd get right on it."

"You believe them?" Doug asked.

His father smiled ruefully.

"I'm sure *they* believe it. Anyway, the premiums were all paid up. I got that confirmed just in case. Maybe we'll get a little back for all that money we've been paying in through the years."

It was clear that Nancy Walker's mind was not on insurance at the moment.

"Do you think I've waited long enough, Carter?"

"Yes. He's had enough time to say what he needed to say by now, I'd think."

Mom gathered her purse, draped her sweater over one arm, and hurried out of the cafeteria, leaving behind a plate of food barely touched. Dad showed no sign of getting up to follow. He was still wrestling with something.

"I don't know what Cat sees in the little twerp," Doug muttered.

His cookie was gone—*inhaled*, his grandmother often described his manner of eating—and his soda was half gone.

"Bad blood between you and Brian?" his father observed, taking another spoonful of soup.

"I know Cat deserves better."

"Your sister knows her own mind, Doug."

"But I know Brian Montgomery. He's an accident looking for a place to happen, and he's found it once too often to suit me."

Suddenly his father seemed more interested. "Reckless?"

"Doesn't think ahead. He doesn't go looking for trouble, but it finds him often enough."

"You two have a history or something?"

29

Doug nodded. "Remember the dent in the car last year?"

"The one Cat put there?"

"The one Cat *said* she put there."

"You're saying she didn't?"

"Brian did it. Brought that old banger of his over to show her. I guess his foot slipped off the brake or something. Grazed our car with the bumper. Cat swore me to secrecy, said she'd take the blame. I agreed at the time, but I don't owe him any favors now."

His father didn't say anything for a couple minutes, letting the spoon rest against the side of his bowl. "I got a call yesterday from someone at the church. Apparently the Montgomerys have retained an attorney," he said out of the blue.

Doug paid close attention now. "Attorney" was not a nice word in his father's vocabulary. It ranked right up there with "politician" and "televangelist."

"What do they need an attorney for?"

"Seems they're wondering what I intend to do about the accident." When Doug didn't appear to understand, his father elaborated. "Wondered if I was planning to sue."

"Are you?"

Carter Walker paused, waited the time it took him to breathe deeply. From long association Doug knew his father was *very* angry at that moment.

"I try not to solve problems by legal action" was all he allowed himself to say.

That explains some things, Doug thought, taking a long last swallow of his soda and crunching the can between his hands.

"Not a word from them for three days, but right after they hire a lawyer, Brian shows up. Just to say, 'Hi, hope you're feeling better,'" Doug grumbled.

"Cynical view of things," Dad commented, though it seemed that he might actually share that perspective.

"Yeah, maybe. I just don't trust those people. Brian especially. And you shouldn't either."

"I'll keep my eyes open," Dad agreed. "By the way, I haven't told your mother yet, but I've decided to take that district manager's position with the company."

This was *not* good news. His father had steadfastly refused advancement from store manager to district manager for the past two years. It meant more money, certainly, but it also involved longer days and even nights away on the road, away from home and family, something he'd resisted. Also it meant pushing paper, something he hated, something for which he had no respect. Doug was sure that it was the thing that his father had been mulling over the past couple days. Instead of asking questions, he kept his mouth shut, let his father continue.

"We're going to need the money, I think," his father finally said.

"What about the insurance?"

"The insurance won't be enough." Carter Walker shook his head. "It isn't supposed to be. It's intended to keep us from financial ruin, not from rough times. Besides, I've had enough dealings with insurance companies to know that there isn't going to be anybody knocking on our door and holding out a check. They don't work that way."

Carter took another sip of his soup, then pushed the bowl away.

"The hospital will bill the insurance company, who will wait a month to pay it. Then instead of cutting a check, they'll send it back because the codes on the billing were entered incorrectly, or because they dispute the procedures, or they need proper authorization, or any of a dozen things. The hospital will resubmit the bill and, after a month and some more delays from the insurance company, will bill us directly and mention very politely how they'd rather not initiate collection. I'll get on the phone, and the insurance company will apologize for the delay and promise to take care of it. Then the next bill will come, and this time there will be finance fees attached as well."

Doug had never heard his father talk this way, never even considered that such tactics existed or were used often enough that people would even suspect that kind of behavior.

"But they've *got* to pay the bills!" Doug said, astonished.

"Oh, they will. Eventually. But everybody will be angry by the time that happens, and a lot of stress will dump down on us all.

When Life Tumbles In

We've got to be prepared to carry the weight until things start moving. And that's going to cost money. It'll take everything that I can make just so we don't lose the house."

Lose the house! Their *home* gone? Doug couldn't believe it. It must have shown on his face.

"That's the way things work, son," his father explained. "It's not right, but the world works the way it works, not the way we think it *ought* to work. And when a man gets handed a challenge, he stands up and faces it. Does what he has to do to take care of his family. Whatever it takes. This is something you need to understand."

"But how can they get away with that?"

"It's not what you think," Dad replied. "They're not 'getting away' with anything. Eventually they'll pay the bills—most of them—anyway. It's just very complicated. Much more so than anyone generally realizes. The paperwork is horrendous, and the government is involved, which makes it even worse, though that isn't what they intended. It's just the way things work. It's better to know how things really work and how to get around the obstacles than to believe something that isn't real and wait for it to happen the way the commercials say it will."

"So . . . you're going to take the district manager's job so we'll have enough to handle the problem?"

"It'll help, anyway. Maybe we can get a loan on the equity in our home. Or perhaps the church can help us. I'll just keep working at it until it's solved."

Doug sat back in his chair. His stomach hurt, and suddenly he was cold. He had never thought about such things before and wondered how his father could just sit there and talk about disaster so calmly. But he knew his father would do just exactly what he said he'd do. A man took care of his family. And Doug knew it was time for him to be a man, too.

"OK, Dad. Then I'm going to help."

His father said nothing.

"The money we set aside for college. Use it if you need it."

"I don't really think . . ."

"Yes, you do. *You* know we're going to need it. *I* know we're going

Putting Away Childish Things

to need it. And I'm willing to put off college to help the family."

Dad looked at him long and hard. Measuring him, Doug realized.

"It may not be putting it *off,* Doug," his father said quietly. "If Cat doesn't get better, if she needs care for the rest of her life, it might mean you *never* get to college unless you earn the money yourself."

"Then that's the way it has to be. Besides, somebody's going to have to take care of things here at home while you're away. Mom will be spending all her time on Cat. Who else will take care of the house and the car and the yard?"

"I've always kind of *enjoyed* mowing the lawn," his father objected with a slight smile.

"If that's how you want to spend your time at home," Doug shrugged, "be my guest. I'll do the rest. Buy groceries, help Mom out . . . whatever it takes," he echoed his father's words.

"Well, we can give it a year and see."

"Fair enough. And since you're not going to be managing the store anymore, you think you might be able to get me a job interview there?"

Dad smiled. "You sure you want to do that?"

"Better something that I at least know a little about. And it'll be more money for the family. A man takes care of his family."

His father nodded, paused a moment, then pushed his chair back from the table.

"OK. I guess I'd better check in on your mother, let her know what we've decided." As he stood up, he reached out and touched Doug's shoulder. "I haven't told you this much," he said, "but I'm proud of you."

Then he turned and left the cafeteria. Both his parents had left their dishes behind. Doug collected the plates and silverware. *Might as well get started,* he thought.

5

A Long, Long Row to Hoe

Doug parked the family car in the driveway next to the company car his father drove and the little Hyundai his mother used going back and forth to the hospital. Setting the parking brake, he turned off the engine and sat there in the sudden silence. The engine ticked as it cooled.

The late-summer night air hung warm all over the city. He'd just returned from saying his final goodbyes to Jill. She was leaving for college in the morning with her parents, a day they had planned together, an adventure she'd now be taking alone.

Jill wasn't happy about the whole thing, and by the end of the evening, neither was he. They'd gone to dinner at an informal little place on the waterfront and sat on the veranda as the stars came out. The breeze off the bay was mild and clean. The lights strung about the dining area twinkled like fallen stars.

He'd tried to explain to her why he had chosen to stay behind, why he'd accepted a position as a cashier with West Coast Drugs at the same drugstore his father had lately managed. She'd remained unimpressed. It didn't seem to make much sense to her, and he couldn't figure out why. The decision made perfect sense to him. Perhaps she felt slighted because he'd chosen his family before her. But that seemed pretty shallow to him, and he knew from experience that Jill was not a petty individual. He guessed it was something he couldn't see, and she couldn't explain. It was mutually frustrating.

But he promised to write. So had she, and they left it at that. She'd be leaving early, and he'd be at work the next morning, still wondering . . . probably.

Doug got out of the car, stretched, and closed the door. As he walked up the path to the front door, he listened to the crickets fill the night air with little creaking sounds. The door was still un-

A Long, Long Row to Hoe

locked, so he locked it behind him. Dad was asleep in the easy chair in the family room.

The remains of a TV dinner and an empty glass of milk sat on a wooden tray next to the easy chair. Dad had a lap table resting across the arms, covered with papers, a calculator, and a laptop computer. The laptop had reverted to its powersave function, and the screen was blank except for a blinking cursor. Jay Leno gestured on the muted television set in absolute silence to an audience—in this house, at least—that couldn't possibly hear him. A lamp shining over the back of Carter's easy chair shadowed his father's face. Everything else in the house was dark. A jacket and tie hung from the back of a nearby armchair.

"Dad," Doug called in a stage whisper. "Dad! Wake up!" He touched his father's shoulder.

For about three seconds Carter Walker had no idea where he was. Doug could see it in his eyes. His father looked tired. Then the man ran a hand through his hair and sat up in the chair in which he'd fallen asleep. "What time is it?"

"Almost midnight. Long day?"

His father nodded, turning off the laptop, the television, and the calculator. "You just getting home?"

"Yup."

"How's Jill?"

"You really don't want to go there," Doug replied.

"Can't be *that* bad?"

Oh, yes, it can be, his son thought. "She doesn't understand why I'm not going to college. Why I chose to stay here."

"Men and women often don't make sense to each other, but the world goes on."

"Mom say anything when she came home?" Doug asked, ignoring his father's sleepy philosophy.

"She was in bed asleep when I got home. Mother needs her sleep. Especially now that Cat's depending on her so much."

"You could use some sleep yourself," his son pointed out.

"Point well taken. On my way to bed."

Dad had just started up the stairs when he stopped suddenly

and came back down. "How's work?"

"Going OK, I guess. Lots of things to remember."

"It does get easier after a while. Beginning anything is hard. You knew that going in."

"I know. Just sometimes I feel kind of stupid."

"Don't worry about it. I've seen this before. All new people go through it. You'll be fine. How's Jerry?"

What his father was really asking had nothing to do with how Jerry, the store manager, was. What he wanted to know was how Doug was working with him. Jerry had been his father's assistant manager, his protégé. Without a doubt he was the hardest working store manager Doug had ever seen. He and Dad were good friends besides being good managers.

"Jerry's great, though I don't have much contact with him. Mostly it's Brent. And he's a jerk."

Dad smiled. "How so?"

"Jerry works right alongside us, shows us stuff. I haven't seen Brent do much more than walk around with a clipboard."

His father chuckled. "If it's any consolation, you've just confirmed Jerry's description of the man too. In fact, that's one of the reasons he's working with Jerry. If he's ever going to be much use to us, Jerry has to whip him into shape. And forget I said that," he added. "Oh, by the way, it's only fair that you know I talked with Jerry about you. I told him not to cut you any slack just because you're my son. Can't have that kind of problem."

Doug shook his head. "I don't think you have to worry about that."

"Good."

A shuffling sound at the top of the stairs drew their attention. Nancy Walker stood in the darkness, knotting the belt of her robe about her waist. The white robe was the only thing Doug could see clearly.

"Carter?"

"Yeah, honey."

"Come to bed."

"OK. Just talking shop with Doug."

"How's Jillian?"

Doug and his father both looked at each other.

"She's fine, Mom."

"That's good. Good night, Douglas."

" 'Night, Mom."

Doug went out to the kitchen and poured himself a glass of raspberry lemonade, something he'd developed an absolute passion for the past few weeks. He had no idea why. The only light came from the moon and the interior of the refrigerator. When he closed the door to the fridge, the moon was all that was left. He sat at the kitchen table, sipping the lemonade slowly in the quiet house. Thinking.

First about Cat. He woke up thinking about her and went to bed still with her on his mind. Wondering how she felt, how all their lives were changing, what the future would look like. He didn't have to share the bathroom with her anymore. Crazy as it sounded, he missed that. No one to blame for the mess but him. No pantyhose dangling from the shower rod. No facial cleansers and body lotions to push aside. His razor looked lonely sitting there next to the sink. And with Jill gone too, that's exactly how he felt. Lonely.

She would leave for college tomorrow, but in his heart she was already gone. And he was still here. Sipping lemonade. In the dark.

"Feeling sorry for yourself," Doug said out loud. "Absolutely right," he answered himself as well.

The clock on the wall, lit by a reflected swatch of moonlight, told him it was nearly 1:00. He had to be at work by 9:00. Setting the glass in the sink, he stared out the window.

"What do we do now?" he asked, realizing a second later he was praying.

Not waiting for an answer, he went straight to bed.

6

Who Your Friends Are

Doug pushed open the door to Cat's hospital room and into a flurry of activity. The evening nurse was just finishing her rounds, doing vitals to pass on to the night nurse. The evening meal sat on a slide-away tray table, special fat-handled utensils neatly placed beside a plate with just a smear of macaroni and cheese remaining. Jean, the occupational therapist, was teaching their mother how to transfer Cat from the bed to the wheelchair and back again using a slideboard. Mom watched as Jean went through the procedure step by step.

"Hi, Jean," Doug said, taking off his coat and gloves.

"Hello, Doug. You're off early."

They were on a first-name basis and had been since Jean had first appeared a couple days after Cat's surgery.

"You're here kind of late, aren't you?" Doug countered.

"No rest for the wicked," she responded glibly. "Just running late. But this worked out well enough. Time you all started learning these things. Cat's not going to be here forever."

"Right," the girl muttered, dragging the bedcovers over her legs. "It just seems like it."

More than a month of hospital food and daily therapy, examinations, and tests, with minimal privacy, were wearing thin on her. Lately she was beginning to snap.

From the beginning Jean had begun working with Cat on her ADLs, activities of daily living. She was teaching her how to eat, how to dress, and how to use the bathroom when much of her body was severely impaired. Jean and Carolyn, her physical therapist counterpart, had tested Cat's range of motion and her level of sensation, mapping the extent of her injuries. And they were extensive, even more so than Doug had feared.

His sister had suffered multiple injuries at varying degrees.

The surgeon, using big words, had explained it all to them. What Doug had gotten out of it was that Cat had experienced a relatively minor injury in the upper thoracic vertebrae, causing a loss of motor control. In this instance, with therapy she would probably regain about 80 percent of her original capacity.

It meant that she could use the large muscles in her arms and have limited use of fine motor control. The injury had mostly affected her left arm and hand, which was fortunate, since she was right-handed. Much of her ability would come back with therapy and training, though she would need to use adaptive tools because her grip had weakened considerably.

However, her primary injury was lower, in the lumbar region that controlled her body from about the waist down. She had no sensation anywhere in her legs. That, as it turned out, was both good and bad. Bad because she would need to examine herself on a regular basis to prevent skin sores and injuries that she could no longer feel. The good part was that in some similar injuries some sensation remained, but that might be limited only to pain receptors. In that case, any sensation experienced the brain automatically interpreted as pain. At least she wasn't constantly hurting.

If Doug wanted to make himself crazy, all he had to do was wonder what it would be like to be injured so and consider how his life would change as a result. Though he tried not to think about it, on dark nights when he couldn't sleep he remembered he'd asked God to spare Cat's life, and it had been spared . . . so she could live the rest of her life injured. Perhaps he should have asked for more . . . or less. Maybe he should have trusted God to do what was right, what Cat needed, and not what he wanted. That was then, he reminded himself. This was now. He hoped someday that he'd be able to let go. The same day Cat walked, probably. Thus never.

"When do I get to go home?" Cat asked, an edge to her voice that Doug had been hearing more often lately.

"Not long," their mother said. "Isn't that right, Jean?"

"Depends a lot on Cat and you," the woman answered, scribbling a quick note in her day planner. "There are skills all of you need to learn so Cat can live a relatively normal life. We also have to check through your home to make things more accessible to her. She needs to be able to do as much as she can for herself. For her benefit . . . and for yours, too."

Jean pushed the wheelchair to the corridor outside the room.

"Another thing we may be ready for is getting her wheelchair measured for her. Do those strength-building exercises I showed you," she said to Cat. "I'll be back tomorrow."

Jean whisked off down the hall. A moment of awkward silence followed, broken finally by their mother.

"See what Cat got?" She held up a wall hanging of an angel wearing a patched and tattered gown. The carefully stitched inscription read: "My guardian angel's a little tattered . . . not as starry-eyed as she used to be. She's been through quite a bit . . . watching over me."

The angel had a starry wand, rosy cheeks, curly hair, and stockinged feet.

"One of the women from church stopped by to see Cat and left this for her."

"One of Mom's friends," Cat said, uninterested.

Doug ran his hand over the material, noting the care taken in the stitching, appreciating the thought behind it.

"Real nice, Mom. Listen, why don't you take a break? Give us a minute here."

His mother looked him in the eye carefully, then nodded.

"I'll just get a soda."

"Good, Mom. I'll be down in a minute."

Doug closed the door behind his mother and paused, then turned around. He saw a bouquet of flowers, obviously handpicked, filling a drinking glass on her nightstand. Odd that he hadn't noticed it before. Cat lay in bed, propped up by pillows, staring out the window at streetlights coming on outside.

"You got something to say?" he asked.

Cat glanced at him, then looked away.

"Come on," he snapped. "You've been taking bites out of everybody these past few days. Let's have at it."

Who Your Friends Are

"I want to go home!" She bit off each word.

"And I want to go to college!" he snapped back. "But it isn't going to happen! Not for a while, anyway," he added more softly.

Cat's face began to crumple, tears leaking down her face. Doug sat down beside her.

"None of us asked for this," he muttered. "We're all just doing what we can do. All of us. So you have to, too."

"Do you remember Wendell DeVere?" she asked, suddenly changing the subject, as she lay there among her pillows.

"Sure," Doug said. "Old guy. Ukulele."

The man was a puzzle to many people Doug's age. He had to admit that before Cat's accident he'd written off the old man as a curiosity. An anachronism. A thing of the past. Of course, not too many people his age had sisters with useless legs who were lying in hospital beds. But Doug's point of view was changing.

"Yeah," Cat said, looking out the window. "Him. He came to visit me today."

Wendell DeVere was an elfin, elderly man who visited those who couldn't do much of anything, for themselves or anyone else. Sometimes with older people his visits involved holding a hand, asking a question about family, or singing an old song while softly strumming his ukulele. For the younger patients, it might be a story, a smile, a bit of verse.

"He sang 'Let Me Call You Sweetheart.' Then he held my hand and told me that God loved me. Not to be afraid." Her voice cracked. "But I am, Doug. How did he know?"

Her eyes glistened in the light of the bedside lamp, and Doug felt cold to the bone.

"What am I going to do, Doug? What's going to happen to me? What's to become of *me?*" she repeated. "Is there anything I can do? Anyone who will want *me* after this?" She gestured at her dead legs under the bedcovers.

Doug swallowed a surge of revulsion, thought for a moment he was going to throw up. Not because of his sister's legs, but because of his own insensitivity. For allowing himself to feel pity for his own troubles. He squeezed Cat's hand and brushed her hair out of her eyes.

7

Holding On

"That'll be $10.79 with the tax, ma'am," Doug said to the little gray-haired woman on the other side of the counter.

"Those aspirin were on sale," she objected.

"Yes, ma'am, but you need the coupon from the ad circular to get that price."

"Coupon? Where does it say that?" she squinted at him.

"Right here, ma'am." Doug unfolded the circular and pointed to the picture. He could read it even upside down.

"I guess I should wear my glasses," she sighed.

"Tell you what," Doug dropped his voice to a conspiratorial whisper. "I just happen to have one of those coupons and can fix it for you if you still want the aspirin."

The woman looked up at him with a myopic blink and a sly smile.

"You know, I don't like all this fine print, but you're a nice boy."

"Thank you, ma'am," he grinned.

After she left his counter, he heard a voice behind him.

"You've got the touch with all the old people," Brent said, standing with a clipboard under one arm. "You finish facing the cosmetic section?"

"No. I've been at the register all day."

"Pull your drawer and count out. Then finish your facing."

"I'm scheduled out in 15 minutes," Doug reminded him.

"Finish the job, then you can go. Any extra time you work today will come out of your shift tomorrow. No overtime."

"OK."

Flipping off his lane light, Doug keyed the shutdown sequence into his register and pulled the cash drawer out, but Brent wasn't through yet.

43

When Life Tumbles In

"Don't think I'm going to cut you any slack because of your father."

The younger man shook his head. "Not a problem."

Brent waved him off, and Doug turned away.

"Jerk," he said, under his breath.

Doug closed the front door behind him with a sigh. The house was dark, no other cars in the driveway. And, just as he had expected, the message machine was blinking with multiple calls. He flipped on the hall light, shed his jacket, and opened the notebook his father had set by the phone.

Pushing the "play" button on the machine, he listened, pen in hand. The first call was from a telemarketer. He knew that because they phoned the house a couple times a day and then hung up when the message machine picked up. He'd taken to hanging up on them, too.

The second message was from a contractor who attended church with them. He was calling to arrange time for the renovations to the house that Jean had recommended when she'd made her home visit. The contractor volunteered to do the job for his own cost as a gesture of fellowship. His father had been speechless with gratitude.

The third message was from Dad.

"Hi, guys. This is Dad. This trip is taking longer than I expected. I'm going to get a hotel and come back tomorrow instead of driving all night. Give Cat a kiss for me, Nance. Doug, be sure to check the oil in your mom's car before you leave for work in the morning, OK? Love you guys. 'Bye."

The fourth message was from a telemarketer, the fifth a fundraiser who promised to call back at a later time, and the last from his mother.

"Douglas, your father called and said he might not be coming home tonight, and I'll be late. Catherine's developed an infection, and she's feeling pretty bad right now. I didn't want to leave her alone. Would you please take the mail in? The insurance people are sending something to us to read and sign. Thanks, honey. See you in the morning."

Doug checked the stack of mail after bringing it back into the house: a bill from the hospital . . . a bill from the anesthetist . . . a bill from the surgeon . . . a sweepstakes flyer from Ed McMahon convinced that they were winners . . . a letter from the insurance company . . . a "3.99% APR" advertisement from some credit card company back East . . . *and a letter from Jill!*

The rest of the mail went on the hall table, where Mom would see it as soon as she arrived home. Then taking Jill's letter, he headed straight to his room, tearing open the envelope as he went. Sitting down on his bed, Doug turned the bedside lamp on, propped himself up against the headboard with his pillow, and shook the single page open.

"Dear Dog," it said, and it was as if he were hearing her voice in the back of his mind.

"Dear Dog, I miss you. I know it's only been a couple weeks since I left, but it feels like forever. Everything moves so fast here at college. My roommate, Carrie, is a dear. She thinks it's funny that I call you 'Dog,' especially since she's planning to be a veterinarian. She's from Spokane. I think you'd like her.

"I'm taking History of Western Civilizations, English Literature, American Literature, German, Tennis, Pauline Letters, and Honors Composition. As you can probably guess, there's a lot of reading and writing involved for 17 credits, but they tell me that's just about right for a first-quarter freshman majoring in English. Fortunately, I don't take every class every day, or there'd be no time to eat or sleep. It's pretty early to tell what the teachers are going to be like, although they all think theirs is the only class I'm taking.

"I'm working as a reader for the English Department. When students turn in their compositions, readers check them for errors in punctuation and grammar. Then the professors read them for content. That way readers get real training doing what they'll be doing later as teachers. I work for Mrs. Stevens, the department head, and for Mr. Wisk, the creative writing specialist.

"I've been thinking about why you decided not to come to college this year. I'm sorry I was so hard on you. Carrie tells me I was . . . well, I won't tell you what she called me. Carrie says what she thinks, which is that you are doing the right thing, and that I should be glad you're a responsible person. And I am. I guess I was afraid of coming here by myself. This sounds kind of silly, but it's true. Like admitting you're afraid of the dark or the monster under the bed. After a couple weeks I know that I'm not going to be eaten or sent home in disgrace because I'm too stupid. Now I can see the sacrifice you've made to help your sister, who's living through a terrible time in her life.

"Please forgive me. I hope that someday you will be as proud of me as I am of you.

"Love, Jill."

He scanned it through quickly, then went back and read it again. When he rubbed the paper between his thumb and forefinger, he felt it crinkle and smelled the tiniest hint of Jill's perfume. As he tried to imagine her in her dorm room at her desk writing to him, he could just about see her flip her long red hair back over her shoulder and out of the way.

The last part of the letter was especially important to him. She had come around after all. Finally she understood why he'd done what he'd done, but then he realized that she'd still gotten it wrong. She thought he was being unselfish, that he'd done all this for Cat. Actually, he'd done it so he could live with himself, and for some reason he was finding that tougher each day. He wanted to be with Jill, not here. Wanted to be taking classes, meeting new people, and getting on with his life.

Her letter had unintentionally turned on a big searchlight into his soul, and it was blinding him.

8
No Place Like Home

Thanksgiving could have gone better, Doug thought as he worked on his knees building a display of cranberry juice cocktail on the front end of an aisle.

Brent had already made one pass by him, warning him to make certain the shelves were secure. He didn't want a display of juice flowing down the aisles. Doug couldn't really blame him. After all, he couldn't think of anything he'd want less either. Unless it was going through another Thanksgiving like the past one.

It was supposed to have been just the family. To be fair, that's how it started, anyway. Cat had finally come home. She'd had to stay in the hospital until the urinary infection was under control. All of the renovations to the house were not yet complete, but at least they weren't continuing to run up bills at the hospital.

They had moved Cat's things from her upstairs room to the guestroom downstairs so she wouldn't have to negotiate stairs. She'd loved her upstairs room because of her view of the bay from her window, but she wasn't sorry not to have to deal with all the stairs. Dad promised at some future date in the current decade to build French windows that would open out onto her own private garden, which did not yet exist either. But it would.

The contractor had removed all the doorframes throughout the ground floor to make the doors wider for easy wheelchair access, but hadn't yet finished. Doug couldn't think of a better way to make a place feel gutted than to tear up every door in the house. But Cat could get her wheelchair through them, so that was the main thing.

"Make sure the labels all face front."

"Huh?" Doug glanced up at Brent.

"Make sure all the labels on the bottles face front," the assistant manager said as he ambled by with his clipboard. "Looks better."

"No problem," Doug replied.

They'd replumbed the guest bathroom so that Cat could transfer easily from her chair to a bench in the shower. Before the accident Cat hadn't needed help with bathing since she was 4. The level of privacy in a hospital being what it was, she hadn't expected much. But at home, washing herself without falling off the bench, and having only her mother to help her, was extremely hard for Cat to deal with. And it wasn't dealt with yet.

Cat had come home from the hospital two weeks prior to Thanksgiving, which was just long enough for the newness of being home to wear off before the holiday. And also long enough for her to realize clearly that being home was not going to solve everything. Yet at the same time it had been long enough for things to get back to as normal as they'd been since the accident. Which meant *not very*.

Retail sales work during the holiday season, which stretched from Halloween past New Year's, was bizarre by any business standards. No one could take any vacations from October 31 through January 1. Managers often worked 10 to 12 hours a day, six and sometimes seven days a week. In Doug's case it involved longer hours and more time with Brent peering over his shoulder as well as the actual holidays of Thanksgiving and Christmas Day, because the chain made a point of being open every day of the year. And it meant delaying Thanksgiving dinner until he could get home.

To complicate matters further, Jill was coming home for the Thanksgiving weekend, and she wanted to spend time with him, too. The plan was for her to have dinner with her own family, then join him after work and share dessert with his family. When had time with Jill, he wondered, become a complication instead of a pleasure? What was changing? More and more often he hadn't a clue.

"You making a career out of that display?" Brent derailed his train of thought.

"Just finishing up," Doug said, stacking the empty cartons on the hand truck. "Here's a list of the UPCs for shelf tags and signs."

No Place Like Home

Brent took the piece of paper with the scribbled numbers, folded it with one hand, and put it in his vest pocket.

"Time you learned how to make your own signs and tags. Meet me back at the computer room in five minutes."

"OK," Doug said, but Brent had already walked off without bothering to wait for his response.

He'd been learning a lot of things lately. But in Brent's case, he wasn't sure whether the assistant manager was teaching him or getting out of his own work. In any case he was learning, slowly but surely.

Jill's visit was surprising. Doug hadn't expected it to be, but it was. Of course, it was wonderful to see her again, to hear her voice, to touch her hand. But something bothered him, something he had trouble pinning down. As she jabbered on and on about her first weeks at college, suddenly he understood. She had been someplace he had never been, done things he'd never done. All through high school their lives had run parallel, but that was no longer the case. Her life was not on hold. No obstacle had deflected it in a direction she hadn't planned. His new experience in retail seemed poor and shallow in comparison with reading Beowulf in Old English, studying Thoreau's thoughts on civil disobedience, tracing the emergence of industry in Europe, or comparing the letters of the apostle Paul.

Vividly she talked about hearing the chimes toll the hour from the belfry of the college church, the notes washing across the countryside and the campus. She described the gold leaves of the oak trees framed against the ad building and the blue fall sky. As she told about the hike up the hill to the Whitman Monument overlooking the historical mission site, her words took on the glow of fairy tales, the Land of Oz, Narnia, and the Promised Land.

The day after Thanksgiving meant something quite different for people in the retail business. It was not another day off before the weekend. Traditionally, it was the busiest shopping day of the year. America consisted of two kinds of people on that day: those who shopped and those who served. Jill was one, and Doug the other.

The store opened early and closed late. By request Doug had

opted for the early shift, figuring to be off by 4:00 and free to spend some unstructured time with Jill until he went back to work Sunday morning, and she returned to college. Naturally, it didn't work out that way.

It was nearly 4:30 before he even got away from his register and closer to 5:00 before he reached home to shower and change. The church had a special service that night, and the plan was to make it Cat's first social event since leaving the hospital. Jill had immediately volunteered to be her escort, which meant, of course, Doug as well. If possible, Doug's father was even later and was just getting into the shower when Jill arrived to ride with them. After some argument, their mother agreed to allow the three of them to go on to church. She and Carter would catch up later.

Mother had gotten so protective of Cat that getting even this small concession was a major achievement. It was either that or the entire family walked in late, and she hadn't wanted to embarrass her daughter with unnecessary attention. She would have gone with them if she hadn't been convinced that her husband would simply get out of the shower and go directly to bed if she wasn't there to properly motivate him.

Doug was the chauffeur, in charge of the car, the wheelchair, and transferring Cat bodily from the back seat to the chair. Both girls sat in the back seat because Jill didn't want Cat to feel separated, so Doug found himself alone in the front driving while they talked behind him.

Getting into church was a bit awkward. Doug had learned how to transfer Cat from the car to the wheelchair, but he hadn't had much practice, since Mom did most of that, and he had never done it in a suit before. Still, as with all new things, it got done, and with Jill leading, he wheeled his sister from the parking lot up the access ramp and through the front doors.

Almost immediately church members crowded about to wish Cat well and tell her how good she looked. And she did, Doug had to admit. His sister was still having difficulty with fine motor control in her hands, but with Jill's assistance and the help of braces that Jean had made for her, Cat had been able to apply much of her own makeup. She was wearing a long peasant dress that draped over her legs, and wore a daisy hairpin just above her left ear.

The girl had missed the start of the school year, but many of her friends attended church, and they quickly joined the well-wishers. The crowd kept them from going anywhere until the ushers helped disperse everyone by encouraging them to find seats. After Doug parked Cat and her wheelchair in a space thoughtfully provided, he sat beside Jill, who stayed next to Cat. When he saw Jill flexing and rubbing one hand, he asked her what was wrong. She explained in a whisper.

"Cat was holding my hand out there and was squeezing it so hard she hurt me. She must have been terrified."

Terrified? he thought. *Of what?*

"It's her first time back in public," Jill whispered again. "First time to be seen. She's afraid. She is scared that none of her friends will want to be around her."

"I don't think she needs to worry about that."

"Just stay close to her when we leave. In case."

In case of what? he wondered. Why did none of this make sense to him?

Vespers began with lowered lights and a tranquil piano solo. The pianist had selected Doug's favorite church song: "Amazing Grace." He had heard it performed a hundred different ways, it seemed, and liked them all. And, though he would never admit it in a million years, once he'd heard it played on bagpipes, he was hooked on that version. It took his breath away.

The pianist had chosen an unfamiliar arrangement, soft, simple, each note like the touch of rain on an upturned face. The song always made him feel better. He closed his eyes and let the music bathe him. At the end of the song he saw to his surprise that Mom and Dad had not yet appeared.

And that wasn't the only problem. Sitting still was making him sleepy. The only thing that kept Doug awake was standing periodically to sing hymns. Otherwise, he found it difficult to keep his eyes focused. It was so much easier just to close them and listen to the pastor's soothing voice.

When Life Tumbles In

Not that the pastor was boring or that he spoke poorly; it was just that Doug had been running since before Halloween, working long hours and odd shifts and constantly changing sleep schedules. Coupled with the soft lighting, the pastor's quiet voice and the comfortable temperature in the sanctuary were more than he could fight.

The elbow in the ribs got his attention.

"You were starting to snore," Jill whispered with a disapproving glance.

"Sorry," Doug said, and he truly meant it. "Real long day."

"I'm sure," Jill whispered back in a tone that left no doubt she expected him to stay awake.

Although he didn't fall asleep again, he didn't get much out of the meeting, either. His mind kept drifting, and by the time the last hymn ended, he was in agony. It was only then that he realized that Mom and Dad had never showed.

It took a half hour just getting to the car while Jill and Cat chatted with everyone after the service. He would have just gone and let the girls talk to their hearts' content, but that didn't seem right somehow. And he guessed Jill wouldn't have appreciated it much either.

Cat was quiet on the drive home, Doug guessed from fatigue. Barely three months since the accident, she had little in the way of endurance yet. She'd been nearly dead weight as he transferred her from the wheelchair to the car at the curb, sliding her carefully into place and buckling her up.

She'd given him a strange look when he fastened the seat belt for her, as if she'd remembered something, but she didn't say anything, and Doug was too tired to press. If possible, Jill was even quieter, but it wasn't from fatigue. He tried several times to catch her eyes in the rearview mirror, but she steadfastly ignored him and stared out the window. Normally it would have bothered him more than it did, but he couldn't dredge up the emotion just then.

Mom was waiting up for them when they arrived. Doug wheeled Cat up the ramp and into the front room. Sitting at the kitchen table sipping a cup of tea, his mother was reading in the silence of the house.

"How was church?" she asked, tightening the sash about her bathrobe and coming over to hug Cat.

"The music was wonderful!" the girl exclaimed. "I had no idea how much I'd missed it."

"We missed you," Jill told their mother.

"I know," she apologized. "Carter was so tired, I just couldn't make him dress and sit in a church pew. He needs his rest. If he'd gone he'd have dozed off and snored."

Jill glanced in Doug's direction.

"Why don't you two run along," his mother said. "Cat and I are headed for bed, I think," she added as she noticed her daughter's drooping eyes.

"Thanks, Mom." Doug kissed her on the forehead. "G'night, Cat. Sleep good."

His sister waved sleepily as Mom wheeled her away. Doug was glad his parents had gotten some time alone. They had almost none together anymore, and every once in a while it showed.

"I'm going home," Jill suddenly announced as Doug closed the screen door behind them. "I'm a little tired."

He understood being tired, but he didn't think Jill meant the same thing he did when he used the word. Exhausted himself, he almost let it go at that. But he sensed there was more involved than just an early evening.

"What's wrong?" he asked, his hand still on the screen door.

"Nothing," Jill said, taking a step down the ramp.

"You've been ticked off at me all evening," he replied, hearing an edge slip into his voice. "Want to tell me why?"

"You could have been a little more enthusiastic about tonight," she snapped. "You *and* your folks. Not to mention Brian. Where was *he* tonight?"

"I couldn't care less where Brian Montgomery was tonight," Doug retorted. "Or any other night, for that matter. As far as I'm concerned, if I never see the little twerp again it'll be too soon."

"This isn't about you," Jill came back at him. "This is about

Cat, and I'm sure *she* was wondering where he was. They *are* friends, you know."

"She doesn't need friends like that."

Jill ignored him, continuing on as if she hadn't heard him at all. "It was Cat's first night out. She could have used his support."

Doug felt his face grow hot.

"This was very important to Cat, but her own parents didn't show, her boyfriend was gone, and her brother couldn't stay awake."

"You know," Doug said, trying to remain calm, "you've probably got good reason to be irritated. I'm sorry you got stuck."

"I wasn't 'stuck.' I volunteered. I wanted this to be special for her, but everybody she cares about let her down."

"Let her *down?*" he asked, his tone incredulous.

Doug knew he should let it drop right there. Nothing good would come of the conversation. He should shut his mouth and nod contritely, whether he felt guilty or not. But he was tired . . . and now he was angry. And he'd never been much good at diplomacy.

"Let me see if I've got this right. You're saying my father, who works 70 hours a week at a job he hates so that we won't lose our home, and my mother, who nurses my sister around the clock, let Cat down because they took an evening for themselves, knowing that my sister would be well cared for? They let her *down?*"

Jill opened her mouth to say something, perhaps to soften her own words just a bit, but Doug rolled right on over her, the anger welling up in the center of his chest.

"I've been up since 5:00 this morning—and a lot of other mornings while most people were still in bed. Where were you at 5:00? Enjoying your rest? Did you go shopping after breakfast? I had a doughnut the manager bought the opening crew. Did you come home later and visit with friends and family while I was standing at a register for eight hours serving people like you? But I dozed off in church and let Cat *down?*"

Her lips formed a thin, cold line.

"Did you notice how tired Cat was?" he asked. "Maybe this whole excursion was too much for her. Or maybe," he paused, "maybe it isn't Cat you're so concerned about."

"Just exactly what do you mean by that?"

He had reached the line—Doug knew it. Anything he said now was over that line, and he was going to pay for saying it. Knowing that, he said it anyway.

"Maybe you wanted to look all concerned and caring to everybody else. You could probably afford an evening helping the less fortunate. What's one night of Cat patrol when you can go home afterward and your whole life is still on track! Well, *my* life is never going to be the same, thank you for asking, but it's *here,* and I'm living it. Cat is part of my life. Maybe I let her down tonight, and if I did, I'll apologize to her. I owe her. But you? I don't owe *you* anything."

Suddenly he felt empty—no anger, no feeling of any kind. He'd dumped it all on Jill, and she was coldly furious.

"I'm going home" was all she said.

"Maybe you should."

And she was gone.

Doug found that he had to sit down on the porch or his knees weren't going to support him. Numbly he wondered where all his anger had come from, and why Jill had ended up being its target. Eventually he'd call to apologize and take a beating for being "insensitive" and "mean." He'd have to eat all the things he'd said to her, and it would be like swallowing glass, but he would do it.

But not tonight.

Maybe not tomorrow. He didn't want to take the chance that some of that anger might still be there, hiding, waiting to pounce on anyone who got close enough. Jill might forgive that sort of thing once, but not twice.

Funny thing was, he was now wide awake.

Doug glanced at his watch as he set the signs and shelf tags on the endcap display of cranberry juice cocktail. It was nearly noon on Sunday. He frowned.

Jill had sat with her parents for church, and he and Cat had

When Life Tumbles In

been with theirs. Never glancing around or making any attempt to see him, she seemed totally focused on the service and the sermon. Later, in the after-service crush, she was nowhere to be seen.

And he hadn't tried to contact her, either, but he wished now that he had. She was leaving for the next few weeks of college before Christmas break. A friend would pick her up, and they would depart at noon.

Somehow he'd hoped she would stop by. Or maybe just phone. He'd have started apologizing the moment he heard her voice. But nothing happened.

The clock swept past noon, and it began to rain.

9
Blue Christmas

Doug couldn't seem to get in the spirit of the season. It wasn't that he didn't have enough time. Christmas decorations had gone up in the store the day after Halloween. Perhaps because he was inundated with it on a daily basis it now meant less to him.

He had written a long letter of abject apology to Jill, shaking his head every time he considered what he'd said to her. She had accepted his apology in a brief note, forgiven him . . . she said. But her letters became quite distant as the Christmas break approached.

The holiday was just five days off now, though he'd done no shopping for presents. The tree was in place because it was artificial, and only the work of a moment to set up. He was planning to get Cat involved with the decorations somehow, but that was another problem. She was having as much trouble getting excited about Christmas as he was.

Of course Doug would be working Christmas Day. He'd made himself indispensable at work, so he was always working. Since he never said no to any project or extra shift, he had a good chance for promotion and even more responsibility. While it meant that he had no life outside of work, that was pretty much the way it was anyway.

Still, Jill's letters disturbed him, and he wondered what he could possibly do to make it up to her. But he wasn't having much luck. Maybe he should talk to somebody. But who? Dad was never home. And he couldn't say anything to Cat without revealing the cause of the problem. He wondered about Mom. She'd proven surprisingly resilient and capable these past months.

Doug was on his way out the door of the store, going home, when he saw it—the perfect gift for Cat. Suddenly the Christmas music didn't seem so smarmy. He dug out his wallet, counted the bills, and decided he'd have just enough . . . if he skipped lunch for a couple days. But the way he was feeling now, it didn't seem like much of a sacrifice.

Doug found his sister in her wheelchair at the kitchen table. Little white boxes of take-out Chinese food sat in the middle of the table. A couple plates smeared with sauce sat in the sink, along with two sets of chopsticks. Cat was shuffling and reshuffling a deck of cards, forcing herself to use both hands.

"Hey, Cat," he said, "what'cha doing?"

"Exercises," she replied, concentrating on getting her left hand to perform exactly as she wanted it to do. "Jean's come up with a new way to irritate me. Ever try to shuffle cards when your left hand won't work right?"

"Nope," he answered, helping himself to a leftover fortune cookie. "Neither of my hands work right. You get enough to eat?" he grinned, indicating the chopsticks.

"Very funny, Doug." She stuck her tongue out at him. "Mom's idea—the chopsticks. More dexterity exercises. And it's almost as much fun watching her eat with them."

In the adjoining room their mother was on the phone using her "business" voice.

"Thank you, no, I haven't been waiting long," and Doug cringed at the tone, "just 13 minutes, 43 seconds by my watch. You must be having a very busy day."

"What's up?" Doug asked Cat, nodding in Mom's direction.

His sister shushed him, wanting to listen, too.

"To whom am I speaking? Cynthia?"

Cindy, Mom, Doug thought. *She probably hasn't been called "Cynthia" since she missed curfew.* Still . . . behaving like a parent might be just the right tack to take.

"I have a problem, and I hope you can help me. In today's mail we received notice from Northwest Memorial Hospital that our bill is in arrears, and they are threatening collection. They say they've received no payments from our insurance company, which is you." She paused, listening to the response on the other end. "Yes, I'm sure it's just an oversight somewhere, but it's important that this be dealt with in a timely manner, so our family's credit doesn't suffer. That would be unfortunate."

Unfortunate for the insurance company, Doug thought. They didn't know his mother, but they were about to learn firsthand.

"I see. You're just the receptionist, and I need to speak to the adjuster. Who would that be? Ah, Mr. Price? Excellent. Please connect me. Oh, I see. No, I don't want to interrupt his meeting, but this is very important. Let me give you all the facts and figures from this end, then you can present them to Mr. Price, and he can call me back."

Cat and Doug listened while their mother rattled off their policy number, the accident claim number, the lengthy list of bills due, complete with their codes and phone numbers, and finally a round figure that accounted for all the money the family had paid in premiums to this particular insurance company through the years. "Cynthia" was going to be swimming in facts and figures. Nancy Walker was nothing if not thorough.

"Oh, and Cynthia, I expect Mr. Price's call on or before 5:00 this evening. If there should be any further delay, I will drive down to your office tomorrow, and my daughter and I will sit in your lobby until we have this settled. Did I mention that my daughter is in a wheelchair? Thank you so much, dear. Have a nice day."

Hanging up, she sighed and came out to the kitchen.

"Eat 'em up, Mom." Doug grinned.

His mother frowned. "I just hate doing business this way, but they asked for it."

"Are we really going to the insurance office tomorrow?" Cat asked.

"Never make a threat you aren't prepared to carry out. Still, I don't think they want unhappy customers cluttering their lobby, honey." Mrs. Walker smiled. "Especially someone so obviously deserving of every courtesy. It's always wise to have a contingency plan in place, just in case. I'd bring along a book, if I were you."

When Life Tumbles In

"They aren't going to know what hit them," Doug said.

Mom smiled at that, pleased with herself and pleased that Doug found it humorous.

"Oh, Douglas," she went on, "there's a letter for you from Jill out on the hall table."

He retrieved the letter, noticing it was quite light. Jill normally wrote often, but not much. A person of few words chosen carefully. These, however, were much fewer words than normal, a lacy note card with just a few lines scribbled hastily.

"Dear Doug, I'll be home again in a few days. I have a couple weeks off for the break, and at some point we need to find time to talk. Take care until then. Jill."

This was not good. The tone was all wrong. Much too brief, even for Jill, and almost . . . terse. He was in over his head, and he had no idea which way to swim. His face must have shown it.

"So . . . how's Jill?" Cat asked.

"Fine." Doug folded the card back into its envelope and forced a smile. "Just fine," he repeated. "She wants to get together during her Christmas break."

Cat flatly didn't believe him, but she didn't push. He was grateful because he had no intention of telling her what the problem was or how it had started.

The telephone rang.

Cat and Doug both looked at their mother. She smiled knowingly and picked up the phone.

"Hello? Oh, Mr. Price. How nice of you to return my call so quickly. Your receptionist, Cynthia, spoke quite highly of you. She said that you could solve my problem if anyone could."

Cat turned to Doug. "Laying it on a little thick, isn't she?"

"Whatever works."

"What's in the sack?" Cat glanced down beside his chair.

"Christmas present for you," he smiled.

"For me?" she grinned back at him. "Can I open it now, or are you going to make me wait for Christmas Day?"

"Suit yourself. Christmas Day doesn't mean what it used to for me," he admitted, taking the package out of its sack.

"You even wrapped it!" Cat giggled.

"Actually, I had it wrapped. The local high school band boosters had a gift-wrapping booth at the store." Doug was the worst of wrappers, and he knew it. When he wrapped a present, it was still visible. Pieces of it anyway.

Carefully opening it, she found a paint-by-numbers kit with extra paints, brushes, and small canvases. Clearly she had not expected it.

"I talked with Jean a while ago, and she mentioned you might enjoy this more than the exercises. I got the brushes with thick handles for you. You can start with the paint-by-number stuff and move on to your own compositions when you want."

"Thanks, Dog," Cat said. She seemed genuinely pleased and more than a little surprised that he'd thought of it. "I appreciate this."

"Glad you like it."

They heard their mother hang up the phone. She looked tired when she sat down.

"Does Mr. Price still have his head?" Doug asked in mock innocence.

"For now. He asked me to send copies of all the billing to him personally, and he promised to expedite matters."

"And you promised to let him live," Cat added.

"Something like that," their mother smiled.

10
Resolution

His head felt as though something was growing inside it, especially behind his right eye. Doug would have sneezed if he could. Sneezing might have relieved the pressure enough so that blinking wouldn't hurt so much. Whatever was clogging his head had set like concrete. There was nothing like a really bad head cold to make one feel mortal.

Pulling the blanket up around his shoulders, he tried to sip grape juice that he could barely taste and focused his good eye on his sister as she sat near the window drawing.

Cat sketched nearly every day . . . or painted. The pleasure she'd gotten from his Christmas gift was the one thing he remembered of the season with real warmth. She'd started with the paint-by-numbers kit, avoiding the pictures with tiny spaces to fill. Cat preferred large washes of color, not so much because they were easier, but because she was not one for delicate detail anyway. Even so, her ability to hold her brushes steady grew quickly.

Soon she went beyond the limitations of numbers and lines. Her first attempt at crossing boundaries came when she reversed all the colors of one painting, creating a color negative of a pastoral scene. Doug thought it resembled a forest glade on Mars.

Next Cat began adding things to her paintings. A collie dog appeared in pointy-toed cowboy boots "just because." A beach scene with frolicking swimmers changed when she added the muted slash of a shark fin in the shadow of a wave. A gaudy sunset slid into satire when she painted a smiley face on the sun.

Finally she abandoned lines altogether, experimenting with pencil and ink sketching, cross-hatching, color mixing, layering, and a variety of mediums. For Doug, observing his sister work was like watching a young hawk take flight. Her eye-hand coordination seemed to improve daily.

Resolution

At her request he'd brought home library books on such subjects as charcoal drawing, water colors, oils, and more. She devoured them. Cat would have spent all day at it had her mother permitted it. Wisely, their mother demanded that she work on her studies each day first. Eventually the girl would be returning to classes, but she had to be ready, and that meant regaining her strength and her motor skills . . . and staying well.

Doug had been so busy at work that he'd paid little attention to what occupied Cat's hours during the day. His "mother of all head colds" had provided him with the perfect opportunity to observe. His only problem was that he'd rather sleep. Still, even semicomatose he'd been surprised to learn of the sheer time and effort Cat required to accomplish simple everyday tasks. Things he took for granted, that he performed without thought, she had to plan and learn and modify.

Just taking a shower had eaten up copious amounts of hot water until they'd installed a simple on/off switch on the removable showerhead. That device allowed Cat to use hot water when and where she wanted it rather than indiscriminately sluicing it over her body as she struggled with the soap. She required less help in the shower these days, but Mom was always hovering close by. Out of sheer frustration with her long hair, Cat had it cut short, almost boyish, so that she could handle more of her own care.

She'd never used obvious makeup, but normal skin care and self-examination consumed major chunks of time each morning. Although nobody ever mentioned how long things took, Doug wondered privately if Cat would ever be able to get herself ready in time to meet inflexible school schedules. Then he pondered why those schedules should be so inflexible. It was something worth thinking about.

Mother made breakfast each morning, but Cat had to feed herself, and she was encouraged to prepare her own lunch. They had to reorganize the refrigerator to eliminate "hidden" food and double stacks. Their mother spent a small fortune on Tupperware containers that Cat could grip easily and open by herself, despite her weakened hands. With her "reacher" device the girl expanded

When Life Tumbles In

her range of efficiency by another yard or so.

After breakfast came schoolwork. Cat proceeded at her own pace through assignments kindly prepared by her teachers and overseen by their mother. But sometimes she had questions on subjects for which Mom had no answers, frustrating them both until Kristen started dropping by. One of Cat's schoolmates, Kristen was a petite, dark-haired girl. Stopping by at least once a week to help with homework, she was particularly good at math. Today she'd glanced in at Doug stretched out on the couch. Cat had explained that he was sick, that they should probably cancel her tutoring just to be safe.

"Get better, Dog," Kristen had said.

He'd waved blearily and gone back to dozing. Much later he remembered the curious look on Kristen's face with some curiosity of his own.

Mom saw to it that Cat took her medications and performed her exercises diligently. The main goal was as much independence as possible, and for Cat that couldn't come fast enough.

What was left of the afternoons was hers once she had schoolwork out of the way. She tired quickly at first and had to take frequent breaks, so sometimes what she did with her spare time was nap. Progress in the beginning was minimal and slow, but it was evident. As it turned out, with a winter both colder and wetter than any in recent memory, Cat's favorite activity was sitting in the sunlight and sketching.

Doug's presence at home altered some things. He ended up sleeping in the family room so that Mom could keep an eye on him, too. His eyes hurt so that he couldn't read. And watching daytime television cost him brain cells, he was certain. Out of pity, Mom had found a radio station that played soft jazz, and Doug drowsed to it.

In between naps he had the chance to consider Jill and her Christmas vacation. Although she had two weeks of holiday, he did not. That was the problem with work. Bosses gave time off only when required by law. With so much to do, it seemed that he and Jill just couldn't connect.

Resolution

Already he could feel the distance growing between them. He berated himself for having allowed his temper free rein. But he also began to wonder if there might be another level to this problem. Maybe he and Jill did not have as much in common as they once had.

The one date they'd managed, a night out with other school friends to bowl and eat pizza, was fun, but they were almost too polite with each other, on their best behavior. It didn't feel very honest . . . or comfortable. He'd always been able to relax around Jill, and now he didn't dare. At times he caught himself dissecting things that she said to him, looking for hidden meanings. It was painful beyond description.

The radio broadcast interrupted its music for a public service announcement about car safety, urging everyone to buckle up, finishing with the tag line "seat belts save lives." At the mention of seat belts Cat stopped sketching. She sat motionless in the thin sunlight streaming through the south windows, her eyes closed, her forehead wrinkled with concentration. Her breathing slowed, almost to a stop. Doug watched, fascinated.

Then Cat took a single deep breath and opened her eyes.

"Welcome back," he croaked.

Blushing, she looked away for a second.

"That radio spot reminded me of something," she said finally.

"Seat belts?"

"Uhmm. I'm remembering more things about the day of the accident."

Doug pushed himself up to a slouched position. "What do you remember?"

She frowned with concentration. "We were headed out on the Hannegan to pick up Brian's cousin. I had a new cassette I wanted him to hear. Alanis Morisette. I remember fastening my seat belt, and Brian insisted I use the shoulder strap, too. You know I hate those. My hair gets caught in them, or they wrinkle my blouse. But I did it . . . then nothing."

"The police said your seat belt wasn't fastened at the time of the accident," he reminded her.

"I know. I don't understand it either, but I remember fastening it. That part's real clear."

"Does Brian remember anything?"

Doug saw that it surprised her that he was aware of her continued friendship with Brian Montgomery. He'd made it no secret of his personal animosity, and Cat had worked to keep the two of them away from each other. She shook her head finally.

"No, and it really bothers him. I probably remember more now than he does."

"Probably because he has fewer brain cells than you do."

Cat ignored the jibe, but she looked troubled. "I just have a funny feeling about all of this, like there's something important I'm missing."

"It'll come back to you, or it won't," Doug said, slumping back down on the couch.

"Profound, Dog."

Cat wheeled past him and out of the room, leaving behind her sketchbook on the end table beside him. Stiffly Doug reached out of his blanket, picked the pad up, and held it close to his face so he could focus better.

It was a charcoal sketch, drawn quickly, roughly, a picture of himself wrapped in blankets, a muffled form with just a hand poking out from under the covers. But instead of drawing him curled up on the couch, he appeared curled in a fetal position in a dog bed, a water dish next to him, his name carefully printed across one side.

In spite of his head cold, he had to smile.

"You got a real nasty sense of humor, sis," he muttered. Then he laid the book down, pulled the blankets up around him, and went back to sleep.

11
Running Away

"Dear Doug," the letter began. "I don't know where to begin."

Jill's letter had arrived just as he'd recovered from his cold and returned to work. He was still a little pale and weaker than he liked, but at least he was on his feet again. Working at the drugstore was like being in elementary school again, catching every childhood disease that came to class. Even Brent had come down with it at some point. Jerry picked up the slack along with whichever supervisor wasn't sick while Brent stayed home. Oddly enough, it was the most pleasant time Doug had spent at work in recent weeks.

Then Jill's letter came.

He had received nothing from her since Christmas, despite two letters he had sent and a phone call intercepted by Carrie, Jill's roommate, telling him she was at the library working on an essay. Carrie had been polite, but vague. Doug had not called or written since.

Now he was holding her letter, the handwriting tight and regimented as if she were marching somewhere, and she wasn't happy about going. It had no nicknames, no little hearts over her *i*'s, no jokes. Just words written in a cramped hand by someone retreating behind formality.

"The past few months have been terribly difficult for you and your family. You're all doing things none of you planned to be doing, and it must be frightening to know that nothing will be the same again.

"The problem I'm facing is that both of us are changing too, becoming different people. At first I thought it was just the accident, the traumatic event that would eventually calm down, become routine. But I was wrong. I have seen a side of you I'd never known before. I've never seen you as angry as you were at

When Life Tumbles In

Thanksgiving. And even though you may have had good reason, it changed how I feel when I'm around you. You've probably noticed that I've been uncomfortable with you since then. I know that you've been very courteous ever since and that it worried you, too, but I didn't know what to say to you that wouldn't make things worse.

"That's why I didn't write for so long. I was trying to decide what to do, what to say, what to feel. That part of you—the angry part—frightened me. I think things have gotten too complicated in your life. You don't know which way to go. I've talked about this with Carrie. She says I can't just let this go on, that I have to tell you how I feel and hope you understand.

"I think we shouldn't see each other, maybe just for a little while. Maybe longer. I don't want to be a complication in your life. And I don't want to face your anger again. College is hard enough for me as it is without adding this kind of trouble to it. This will simplify things for us both, I think. Maybe things will change. Get better. We can always hope.

"Carrie says I have to be completely honest with you. This isn't all your fault. I've met someone else here. I really like him, and we have a lot in common. I want to get to know him better, but I can't do that without letting you know how things stand.

"I would like to go on being friends with you, but I will understand if you don't want me around. This hasn't been easy for me, either. I hope you have a good life.

"Sincerely,

"Jill."

Doug balled the letter up in his hands, bounced it off the wall, and heard it plunk into the bottom of the garbage can. Later, he guessed, he'd retrieve it, smooth out the wrinkles, and read it again. Then, after he had committed it to memory, maybe he'd burn it for good measure.

But at the moment he needed to get out, to do something.

Changing into sweats and running shoes, Doug became absorbed in lacing his shoes just right. His mind was a seething blank, as when a closed door mutes the sounds outside a room.

Running Away

He knew he was feeling something, but he didn't want to look at it too closely, afraid of what he might find.

The women in his life always wanted to know what he was feeling. Introspection seemed a waste of time to him. He "felt" hungry or tired, strong or sick. When he was angry or sad, it was more an action than a feeling, but that didn't make much sense even to him. How could he expect anyone else to understand?

He pounded down the stairs, only to be caught at the back door by his mother folding clothes.

"Douglas, where are you going? It's almost dark."

"Mom!" he said, not wanting to talk with her. Not now. Most especially not now. "I've got to go . . . for a while. Somewhere else."

His mother stared at him, and he couldn't look back. She'd see the pain and want to comfort him. And he didn't want comfort. He wanted to hurt, to crash headlong into walls and bleed and rage and feel the strength of the darkness in his chest. No, he didn't want anyone else to see what was raging inside him.

She touched his shoulder gently, and it was all he could do to keep from screaming at her. Her empathy, her love for him was a torment to him. He had to get out.

"Be safe" was all she said as she opened the door.

Gritting his teeth, he ran into the gloom.

Doug hadn't touched the bicycle since Cat's accident, and he didn't want to be on the street biking in the dark. But he could run. And he did.

Civic Field was only four or five blocks away. It was an open track flanked by bleachers along the front and backstretches, and he reached it as the light began to fail. Doug ran one circuit before the drizzle settled in. He barely felt it. On the second lap he fell into a comfortable rhythm, his shoes making a crunching sound on the track. His breathing began to labor near the end of the third lap, but he started to hope that if he could just keep running, he might be able to burn the pain out of his skin.

Eventually he lost count of how many times he had circled the track. All he could feel was the fire in his chest, the watery sensation in his legs. Streetlights cast a pall onto the field area as he

When Life Tumbles In

ran. His pace suffered, began to slow, until it was little more than tortured stumbling. Doug slipped on wet grass, realized he'd actually left the track, and halted against the bleachers.

Sitting down, he closed his eyes and heard Jill's voice. Felt her touch. Smelled the perfume in her hair. Then he turned his head suddenly, a spasm, and vomited out the darkness inside him. His face was wet, but it was probably the rain.

12

Dark of Night

When he finally made his way home, the house seemed quiet. Dad's car wasn't in the driveway . . . no surprise there. Doug slipped in the back way, hoping to avoid everybody, but Cat was waiting for him at the foot of the stairs. Mom was in the kitchen shuffling pots and pans around, making cooking noises. Even so, Cat still pitched her voice low so that their mother wouldn't hear.

"It's Jill, isn't it?" she asked.

He considered telling her a lie, but standing there in sweats dark with rain, his hair plastered to his head, his hands fisted and beginning to shake, it seemed somehow like too much effort.

"Yes," he nodded. "She met somebody else."

He'd never tell her how it had all come about, but she had already guessed most of it. Maybe he wouldn't have to say anything more.

"You better get into some dry clothes," Cat said. "Mom will have a cow if she sees you dripping on the carpet."

Despite himself, he smiled, a bare tugging of one corner of his mouth. Cat saw it and smiled back before wheeling away down the corridor. Doug climbed the stairs, his knees trembling, and the cold from the rain like a vise on his body.

A hot shower got rid of the shakes. The anger was gone too, the rage washed out of him. But sadness left him weak and empty. Doug let the hot water batter him, streaming over his shoulders and down his back and legs. He breathed in the cloud of warm mist, and though his body grew warm, a part of him still remained cold in a way that no hot water was likely to thaw.

Afterward, it was all he could do to towel himself dry. He just wanted to sit on the edge of the tub and stare at his face in the mirror. Somehow he'd changed and was too different for Jill to love him anymore, ever to feel comfortable around him. But

When Life Tumbles In

another thought lurked behind those bruised eyes in the mirror. He wondered for the briefest of moments what he'd ever seen in her.

Dad had come home while he was in the shower. Mom had cooked up macaroni and cheese, the kind he liked, with extra cheese oozing everywhere. Frozen veggies and garlic bread rounded things out. Dinner was quick and easy. They had all gotten good at that—they'd had no alternative. The kitchen was lively, with everybody talking except him. He was a silent island in a sea of conversation, eating and listening, then going to bed early.

Strange, he thought. The running had sapped the anger right out of him. He should have been upset, but he had to admit as he lay under the covers that nothing much mattered to him. Even Brent seemed relegated to the status of mere nuisance. *Maybe,* he thought, *I should run more often.* Doug was considering the idea when sleep finally overcame him.

His sleep seemed to be dreamless, but he did wake up with the sky still dark. For a second he felt a brief twinge of sorrow, but it was manageable. He wondered how Jill was feeling. Then he decided that he could use his energy better.

Quietly he went downstairs, his legs protesting mildly, and peeked in at Cat asleep soundly with the blankets pulled up over her shoulders. After listening to her breathe in and out, he then went on out into the family room to sit in the bay window and watch the night.

He wanted to talk to someone, but he didn't know to whom or what exactly he'd say, so he just sat. A light breeze in the branches of the trees along the street brushed shadows back and forth across the light thrown by street lamps. It was as if the trees had come alive in the darkness and were conversing. Without realizing how he'd started, Doug caught himself talking to God.

But not praying. He hadn't prayed to God since his sister's accident. He wasn't sure where he and God stood in their relationship—wasn't sure he wanted to know. Instead, he decided just to talk, and if God wanted to, He could listen. Strangely enough, it felt almost natural.

Not that he was letting God off the hook—not by a long shot. He'd asked Him to spare Cat's life, and He had, but He'd left her disabled. It wasn't right. She didn't deserve it. Getting cold, Doug snagged the afghan off the back of the couch, draped it around his shoulders, and sat back down in the bay window.

Nothing made sense anymore. Why had God protected him that day on his bike, but He'd allowed Cat to be injured in a car accident? Why was his father being pulled away from a family who loved and needed him? Was his mother's sole purpose in life to be his sister's nurse? Why was his chance at college snatched from him? All their lives were changing. What was the purpose in that?

The big family Bible sitting on the end table by the sofa reminded him of a game he and Cat had played when they were children. They would open the Bible randomly, close their eyes, and then place a finger blindly on a text, pretending it was God's message at that moment for them.

Smiling to himself, Doug retrieved the Bible, closed his eyes, and found just such a text at random. It turned out to be in the story of Job, in which God answered Job's questions by reminding him whom he was questioning.

"Where were you when I laid the foundations of the earth . . . decreed the boundaries of the seas . . . commanded the morning to appear?" Doug read.

But he was not Job. It made him furious.

"That's not going to work," he hissed. "I'm not going to be intimidated by that. If You're the parent, and we're all the children, then You're responsible for us all. It's Your job to bring us up right, to keep us safe. And lately You're not doing so well."

He didn't get an answer, and he really didn't expect any. On television or in a story, this would be the point when an angel would appear and move the plot along. But no angel came to him. He wondered why no one saw them anymore. Why were there no burning bushes, no parting seas? Didn't people need miracles anymore? Had God abandoned them? Or had something changed? One thing was certain—the last time he'd asked God for help, he'd done something wrong, and his sister was paying the price. That made it really difficult to pray to God, to accept His authority. Doug believed in God—he just didn't trust Him.

"You're up kind of early," his mother surprised him from the doorway. Her hair was already brushed and orderly, even though she must have just gotten up.

"Woke up and couldn't go back to sleep."

"You were really upset about something yesterday. Catherine wouldn't say anything. Did you want to talk about it?"

Doug followed her into the kitchen where she put water on to boil for tea and hot cocoa. He didn't like hot beverages, but Mom would throw a fit if he had a soda this early, so he'd settled for cocoa.

"I don't know what you can do about it," he said, settling into a chair at the table and draping the afghan over his shoulders again.

"Maybe I can't do anything, but I can at least listen."

He shrugged. "Jill and I had a big fight during Thanksgiving, and we didn't get it solved during Christmas. I just got a letter yesterday saying she'd met someone else."

"Oh, Douglas," his mother sighed. "I'm so sorry."

She sat across the table from him, and to his surprise he saw tears in her eyes.

"I'm not going to tell you there are other fish in the sea," she said. "Jill's not a fish. You have good reason to be upset. It's normal. And it's very hard to maintain a relationship over a long distance."

Doug got up when the water in the kettle began to whistle. He poured most of it into a waiting teapot for his mother and the rest into a cup of cocoa powder.

"You and Dad seem to do all right," he pointed out.

"Well, it's a bit different for us," she said, steeping the tea while Doug stirred his cocoa. "We're older, for one thing, and we have a bit more experience making a relationship work."

"But you had to start somewhere. How did you guys know this was forever?"

His mother sipped her tea before answering.

"We didn't," she said finally. "We took time to get to know each other. Love isn't chemistry."

It was half of her favorite saying.

"It's hard work." That was the other half. Doug smiled with recognition.

"But in the beginning, we didn't know it would be forever. Maybe that's not very romantic, but it's true. Who can know that? We took a chance that we could make it work. A leap of faith, I guess."

"I thought Jill was the right one for me."

"Did you ever talk about marriage?"

"Some. Mostly that we should do college first. I just assumed we had the time to work the rest of it out."

"Your father and I talked about everything. We still do. Marriage isn't just a word, but words can help."

"It's still got to be hard for you and Dad."

"Sure," Mom smiled. "If it were easy, everybody would do it. But I have no doubt your father loves me . . . and both of you."

"That must be a good feeling." Doug sat back in his chair, warming his hands with his mug of cocoa.

"It's the best kind of feeling," she agreed.

Dad entered the kitchen just then, tying his tie as he walked. If anything he looked more preoccupied and disturbed than usual. He stopped, however, and kissed Mom on the top of the head before rummaging in the dish drainer for a clean mug.

"What's up?" Doug asked.

His father almost didn't answer, but then appeared to change his mind.

"Can you keep a secret?"

Doug nodded.

"The chain is in negotiation to merge with a large East Coast drugstore conglomerate called Sharpe's. And we're not the ones initiating the buyout."

"What does that mean?" Mom asked.

"It means we won't be making the decisions any longer. They will. Usually the first thing that happens is that the parent company eliminates duplicate support personnel and the exec-

When Life Tumbles In

utives of the smaller company. Depending on how far they go down the corporate ladder, I may be out of a job."

Doug sat stunned. He'd never considered that possibility.

"It's always just one more thing," his father said.

13
Breaking Point

Being fairly low on the corporate food chain did have some advantages, Doug decided. If all you wanted was a job, it didn't really matter who owned the company, at least at his level. Work still had to get done, and there had to be people who did it. When the East Coast representatives of the new owners came to tour their new holdings, all he had to do was keep his head down and his mouth shut. They weren't interested in him anyway.

But as the district manager, his father wasn't so lucky. He had to ferry them from store to store, and Jerry and Brent had to "walk and talk" with them as they studied the layout of their store. Making a good impression should have been easy enough. Jerry knew his figures. The store was clean and busy, had its plans in place, and had a good cash flow.

Still, the little exposure Doug had to the new bosses led him to believe they were singularly unimpressed. They intended major changes, they boasted, and everybody "had better get on board." Their visit didn't win them any friends.

Despite the fact that East Coast stores in the chain were small and primarily urban and that the West Coast units were literally four times the size of their counterparts and suburban, the new owners intended to clone the East Coast designs, and they weren't afraid of major surgery to get the job done.

Financially borderline stores would close, the employees parceled out to other locations or laid off. New hires came in chained to minimum wage as part-time help, saving the new company from contributing to benefit and retirement programs. Profitable stores faced downsizing and high-tech refits that required fewer employees to run. Unfortunately, the rumors flooding in from other stores warned that the new management was pushing the transition so fast that any glitches were being fixed ad hoc during the installment phase. When there were problems and the refits failed, the stores did not have enough staff to handle the crises.

Morale began to plummet both at the store and at home. Carter Walker was not a happy man, and it showed in his growing preoccupation. He was not in love with his position as some district managers were, but he took pride in his work, in a job well done. The new people wanted the job done their way and immediately, but they kept setting limits on how his father could do it. And they didn't want to hear any "excuses."

Mr. Walker handled the stress internally, growing quieter, sleeping less, and eating sporadically. Jerry was openly hostile toward the "reps" from the new company, unafraid to point out the myriad flaws in their plans and fully expecting to be summarily terminated for his arrogance. Brent, however, bought into the new concept completely, and when they missed deadlines for any reason, he took out his frustration on the crew. People began to quit, and the new hires coming in to replace them required training and careful supervision.

Doug soon found himself one of the most experienced employees left. He received a small raise and a lot more responsibility. If possible, Brent was on his case even more than before.

One afternoon in the Camera Department as he hunched over the keyboard of the Western Union access station, he called for assistance to handle the growing line of customers, and no one responded. He was trying to find a particular money transfer for a distraught woman and her kids. Stranded by transmission failure, they were waiting for money to repair the car. Western Union shared a phone line with the pharmacy fax machine because it was less expensive, but since the pharmacy had priority, Western Union routinely got bumped of line when things became busy. On this particular day the fax machine had cut him off twice already on this one transaction.

At Doug's third call for help, Brent appeared with his clipboard, taking in the situation with one irritated glance. Doug continued pecking away at the keyboard while the assistant manager took care of the other customers.

"What's the deal, Walker?" Brent demanded when he was finished. "Why didn't you ask for help?"

"I called three times."

"Never heard you. We got people standing around up front. Why didn't they come if you called?"

"Ask them," Doug retorted.

"Watch yourself," Brent pointed a finger at him. "Don't let things get so far out of control next time."

Then he left.

The woman Doug had been helping looked sympathetic. "What a jerk," she said.

Running saved him.

If he ran early, before working a later shift, his head seemed clearer, his level of patience pushed up a notch. And if he did it after working a full day, the stress and anger drained out of him like sweat.

Kneeling beside the track, he'd tie his running shoes tight and take several relaxing breaths. It didn't matter, though. He couldn't really relax unless he was in motion. The first few steps always felt clumsy, painful, and always he heard a voice inside his head say, "This is stupid." It was his own voice—he recognized it—his body literally dragging its feet. "This is really going to hurt," it complained. Soon he started talking back, though he was careful to keep the volume down when other runners were on the track. "Gotta run," he'd say, gritting his teeth. "Got no choice. Gotta run."

His inner voice grumbled through the first lap, but then the noise of his running drowned it out. He could hear the crunch of the track surface under his feet, the rush of wind past his ears, the bellows roar of his lungs, and near the end, the pounding of his heart.

As his muscles loosened up, his legs and arms began swinging in a rhythm, and the tightness in his stomach eased. He could feel warmth spreading out from his heart and lungs. His sense of smell became more acute.

Some people, he'd heard, ran to clear their minds so that they could think. He ran so he could stop thinking. There was a point when the immediacy of the pain and the pleasure of running shut out the outside world. Nothing beyond the track existed. There was only breathing, his arms swinging, and his legs eating up ground. It was a wonderful place.

The first time he had started carefully, not wanting to overdo things too early. He had stretched and moved out slowly, walking before easing into a jog. That first week he had run only a mile each day, but he found himself wanting more. He guessed that was a good sign. The next week he added another mile, and a third mile the week after that.

Some days he ran even more, and as the weeks passed, he found his pace increasing, his distance expanding, and his peace of mind growing. Eventually he ran in the rain, in the sun, in the wind, and in the dead, clear calm. He drank water to keep hydrated and layered his clothing to adjust to changes in the weather.

When he couldn't run, he became irritable. It was like an itch he couldn't scratch. Most of the time he ran alone. Often he saw other runners on the track, but they were all a bit solitary, so it was not uncommon to speak to no one when there were half a dozen people circling the track at their own paces.

That's why it was a surprise when a young man drew up next to him as he was heading into his fifth mile.

"Hi," the individual grinned, his voice a bit breathless.

Doug nodded back, polite, but only barely. The other runner was slight and dark, sweat stains coloring the loose shirt he wore. He looked familiar, but Doug couldn't place where he'd seen him before.

"I'm Jase. How's your sister doing?"

It was like hitting a wall. Doug dropped down to a shambling walk.

"How do you know my sister?" he demanded.

Jase smiled wide and deep. "I work at the hospital."

"Little young for a doctor," Doug snorted.

Jase was more his sister's age.

"Nothing like that," the young man shook his head, "although my brother works in the Physical Therapy Department."

Doug was cooling off rapidly. He untied the sweatshirt from

around his waist, tugged it over his head, and kept walking.

"I work at the espresso stand in the lobby. You know, Thirst Aid? After school. You bought a latte from me a couple times."

"For my mother," Doug corrected him.

"Ah" was all Jase said.

"So . . . out of all those customers, you remember my sister that you'd never met—and me?"

"Heard about her accident from one of the ER techs, and I dropped by once or twice with a flower for her."

Strange, Doug thought. *Cat never even mentioned that.*

"I'm OK. Really," Jase assured him. "I'm not a stalker or anything. Just recognized you out here, and I was hoping your sister was doing better."

"Still disabled," Doug replied tersely.

Most people would have gotten the message and left well enough alone, but Jase was not "most people."

"Only her body," Jase grinned, then picked up the pace and moved off, leaving Doug standing on the track.

He nearly forgot to mention the chance encounter to Cat. Although he had fully intended to tease her about it when he got home, the sweat cold on his body, he heard his parents arguing in the kitchen.

"It can't be helped!" his father was saying.

"It's got to be," Mother snapped. "Carter, you have spent exactly three evenings this past month in this house. And one of them you spent in front of your e-mail laptop putting out fires instead of talking with your children and me."

"That's what it takes," his father insisted. "I had to interview for this position, did you know that?" he asked angrily. "I have 30 years' experience in retail at all levels, and they wanted me to know they expected my *best* effort. That younger men were just itching to run with this up-and-coming corporation, and my work was cut out for me. I have to be faster, more efficient, harder working, *and* smarter than all their East Coast cousins who want to work for 'uncle' and make names for themselves. If I slow down, they'll run right over me!"

"Then it's time to get out!" she pleaded. "We need to see more of you."

"Let's be real for a minute," he said, exasperation in his voice. "I hate working for these people. They're amateurs making mistakes we solved years ago, but they don't know that, because most of the people who knew those solutions either quit or were laid off because they weren't 'essential.' We need the money. You know that—you see the bills! We're maybe three or four paychecks from the street, despite our savings!"

"Carter!" she shushed him. "The kids!"

"You think they don't know this?" His father sounded incredulous. "Why does Doug run? You ever ask yourself that?" The man sounded like he was close to tears from frustration. "He's out there running for his life. Running's the only thing he's got some control over. And he understands what we're facing. Perfectly."

By now his mother was crying. His father went to put his arms around her, but when she backed away, he dropped his arms to his sides, helpless.

"Carter, I understand what you're up against. But it's not just you. I love Catherine and Douglas. I'd do anything for them, but I *miss* you. Douglas tries so hard to *be* you, and when he can't, he *runs*. Catherine thinks all of this is *her* fault. Our family is falling apart," she said desperately. "I can't hold it together alone. I *need* you. I don't have an answer. I just know *this* isn't working."

Mr. Walker pulled out a chair at the kitchen table and sat down.

"I don't know what to do," he said finally. "I don't know how to fix this," he concluded miserably.

Doug's mother sat next to her husband and took his hand in hers, leaning against him, sitting there in the kitchen in silence.

As he backed down the hall, Doug was glad he hadn't been noisy coming in. He nearly fell over Cat, who'd been listening from the back of the hallway. She was scowling.

"It's getting worse," she said.

"It'll be all right," he reassured her.

"It isn't all right!" she hissed back at him. "It's all coming apart."

"Listen, Cat, parents argue. Life is hard. We go on. There isn't any other option."

"But I caused this."

Her eyes were dark and watery. Doug thought it might be possible to drown in them.

"Did I ever tell you what happened to me the day you were hurt?" he asked.

She didn't seem to be listening.

"I came this close"—he held up his hands to measure the distance—"to being hit by a car. It could have been me in the hospital just as easily—or both of us. We could be dead. Whose fault would it have been then?"

He watched a tear cut down his sister's cheek, then patted her hand clenched on the arm of her wheelchair. It was hard as rock.

"Better if I'd died."

That scared him. Partly because it meant she'd been thinking about that, and partly because it was something he'd also wrestled with in the middle of dark nights.

"Don't say that, Cat."

"Why? It's true."

He looked her in the eye. "Because I couldn't bear it."

Only then did her hand soften, her shoulders shaking as she sobbed in great, heaving silent shudders. As he patted her hand, looking about in vain for a tissue, he realized that he was crying, too. *This is stupid,* he thought. *And messy.*

"Met a secret admirer of yours," he said, desperate to change the subject. Not sure that she heard him, he continued, "He said he left you flowers in the hospital."

Her eyes came up.

"He wanted to know how you were. Ran me down at the track just to ask me that."

She sniffled, and then the oddest expression crossed her face.

"I didn't say anything about it," she admitted. "Thought you'd make fun of me."

"And I will," Doug promised.

"You think maybe I could go with you the next time you go running?"

"Sure," her brother said, and smiled.

Doug hitched a ride to work with his father the next morning, deciding to take the bus home at the end of the day.

"Dad," he began as they left the driveway, "Cat and I heard you and Mom arguing last night."

"Don't worry too much about that, son," he said with a dismissive gesture. "Married people argue from time to time. It's normal."

"We know that, but Cat and I still think it's important not to let things ride."

"I don't understand," his father said, signaling to turn and looking for oncoming cars before pulling out into the intersection.

"Cat and I think you're both right. You aren't around enough, but the demands on your time aren't going to ease off, not with this merger. If something's going to change for the better, we're going to have to *make* it happen. Not *wait* for it to happen."

Dad smiled faintly. "What did you have in mind?"

"How much vacation time do you have coming?"

"Four weeks. But I couldn't go away for a month."

"Not a month. Just a weekend. You and Mom. That's what she was really saying, you know."

"I know," he agreed. "Your mother's a fine woman. She deserves better."

"She deserves time with *you*. And you need to get away with *her*. Cat and I understand."

"You do, huh?" his father grinned at him, then checked the rearview mirror. "What about you two?"

"We can take care of ourselves for one weekend. Really. You can call if you absolutely have to. Cat's getting pretty self-sufficient. I can get some time off. They owe me. I can take care of anything she can't."

"You're pretty confident."

"I was taught by the best."

His father was quiet for a moment. Doug almost said something, but the older man spoke first. "I'll talk with your mother."

It took another week of planning, but their parents got a weekend to themselves. They decided to drive along the coastline and stay in small hotels along the way, buying groceries instead of eating out. Mom had always loved the ocean, and Dad loved Mom.

Still, they almost didn't convince her to leave Doug and Cat by themselves. That hadn't been her idea at all. She was a phone call away from asking Gramma to come up from Salem and baby-sit them. Cat had taken her aside and talked hard and fast. Finally she'd agreed, promising to check in every evening by phone.

"It's going to be only two nights!" Doug protested, knowing he'd lose this argument.

"Best deal I could get," his sister tossed at him. "Be happy."

Doug guessed it didn't really matter that much. He could live with it.

Their parents left late Friday afternoon, planning to drive only a couple hours and get to bed early. Jerry had agreed to pick up the slack for his father for a couple days. Privately Doug thought most of the corporate whiners out there wouldn't bother calling, knowing it was Jerry on the other end of the line instead of his father.

Their parents waved as they pulled out of the driveway, Mom calling suggestions as they backed out.

"Mom!" Cat shouted. "Go away!"

She laughed and rolled up the window. Then they were gone. Doug pushed his sister back up the ramp and onto the front porch.

"So, Skipper," she turned to him, "what do we do now?"

"Well, little buddy," he smiled, "now we party!"

14

Thin Ice

"Not that kind of party," Doug protested, seeing the expression in his sister's eyes. "The strongest thing at this party is going to be my aftershave."

"OK, so what are we talking about here?"

"Good food, good people, good music," Doug suggested. "Maybe some video games, a movie, whatever you want. Doesn't have to be big and noisy to be a good party. Besides, I don't want to have to explain anything to Mom and Dad when they get home. No rowdies allowed."

"Can I invite whoever I want?"

"Your party. I'm just the enforcer."

"And pizza?"

"As long as I get some."

"May Brian come?"

Surprisingly, Doug didn't immediately feel sorry he'd proposed the idea. He was making progress, he thought.

"Just keep him away from me."

"Done. When do we do this?"

"Saturday night OK?"

The light in Cat's eyes warmed his heart—he'd forgotten he could feel this way.

Doug had never written back to Jill to answer her "Dear Doug" letter. He'd started a couple times, but had degenerated into wordlessness before the end of the first sentence. It wasn't as if they'd been engaged or anything, he reminded himself. She could see anybody she wanted. For that matter, so could he. But thinking about meeting someone new was like being hungry and finding the fridge full of broccoli. He wasn't *that* hungry.

Finally he realized there was no point in writing back to her. And he found himself oddly relieved. Sure, he now had a hole in his life, a void where there used to be something wonderful. But he was getting used to that anyway.

Running filled his free time, but he didn't do it because it was fun. It was more like eating or sleeping—something he had to do to survive. He hadn't done anything fun since Christmas. Maybe while Cat was having her party he could somehow also enjoy himself.

Most of the kids she invited over were from church, a pretty decent bunch generally. Although a little heavy on the female side, that was fine with him. They arrived singly or in twos as it began to get dark. The pizzas were ready, the video cued up, the music playing—a tad too "Backstreet Boys" for him—but it was Cat's party.

She'd managed dressing herself, blue jeans and a denim shirt with a vest all in butterflies. Doug had helped her comb her hair back, but being as short as it was, that was more a formality than a necessity.

Things started off well. He skirted the edge of the party, a can of soda in his hand, watching her friends play charades, including her in the game as if she weren't any different. Funny that he was the only one who seemed aware she was disabled.

Then he saw Brian pull to the curb, and a blond girl got out of the passenger side. The first inkling that he was going ballistic was a rush of heat to his face and chest that made him feel as if he could smash through walls. Brian had no idea what he was walking into.

Fortunately, Doug had the presence of mind to go out to meet him and his date instead of confronting him in the house. The screen door slammed behind Doug like a gunshot, and he strode down the ramp, his fingers and toes cold as ice.

"Dog!" Brian said, a smile fading from his face as he realized Doug was blocking the entrance. "What's up?"

"You got nerve," Doug bit off his words.

"Huh?"

Brian's date was smarter than he was. She didn't approach any closer. As usual, Brian hadn't a clue.

"You *know* how much my sister cares about you," Doug snapped.

"What are you talking about? I care about her, too."

Doug took a handful of Brian's jacket, not pushing, not pulling, just holding. He stepped in close, right in the kid's face.

"Cat invited *you* to a party," he said quietly, coldly, "not you and your date. You're *not* bringing your new girl in there. Not while I'm standing here."

Relief flooded the boy's face, surprising Doug.

"Teri's my *cousin!*"

"Teri?" Somehow Doug forced his fingers to open, releasing the boy's jacket.

"Right! Cat and I were headed to Teri's house when the accident happened. She always wanted to meet Cat, and when I was invited I asked if Teri could come too."

Mortified, Doug felt the anger drain out of him right into the ground.

"Doug, I'd never hurt Cat on purpose. You have to believe me."

As Doug looked into Brian's face he recognized the misery he found there.

"I'm the reason she's the way she is," he went on. "I made a mistake, and she's paying for it. I can't ever forget that, even if I wanted to. As long as Cat's in that chair, I will be too."

His face burning, Doug nodded, ashamed. "I'm sorry," he said. "I couldn't let anything else hurt her."

Brian put a solemn hand on Doug's shoulder. There was nothing to be said, and for once Brian was wisely silent. Doug mumbled an apology to Teri as well, and when they went in to join the party, he stayed outside for a while, resting his head against the side of the porch beam. He was out of control and didn't know what to do. Jill had been right after all. Sooner or later something bad was going to happen.

Another fine mess, he sighed.

Cat never found out about the incident on the porch from Brian, and Doug was grateful. He owed the boy. And wasn't *that*

a strange new feeling. It was bad enough that his anger had cost him his friendship with Jill. Now he risked disappointing Cat as well. Subdued the rest of the evening, he was content to let his sister enjoy her party and her friends. Doug hung back, watching, taking care of the food, bringing out games at request, cleaning up afterward.

The party seemed to energize his sister as she drew strength from the contact with her friends. As for himself, he was oddly calm at evening's end. He'd done most of the cleaning, with Cat assuming the role of host, thanking everyone for coming, joyfully accepting their hugs and touches, sharing a sly look with Kristen.

Kristen had shown more than a passing interest in Doug the entire evening. She had managed, without graceless fawning, to be near wherever he was, helping him distribute the root beer floats they'd had for dessert, clearing away tables after games had concluded. Once he had turned suddenly and nearly fallen over the girl. Although Kristen had blushed just like Cat, it hadn't stopped her from staying close to him.

And Cat was never going to let it lie.

"She's a little young," he said, by way of forestalling the teasing he was certain was coming.

"Just because you see her that way. She's two years younger than you. Mom and Dad are five years apart."

"Yeah, and millions of years older, too."

"I'm going to tell them you said that."

"Careful. I'd have to let it slip about the party, how much trouble you and your friends got in. Disorderly and disrespectful, all of you. Trashing the house and scaring the neighbors," he grinned.

Cat laughed, and his heart leaped at the sound. "That story's so lame it needs this chair more than I do."

She'd changed into her nightgown, and he helped her into bed, tucking the covers up under her chin. When she immediately pushed them off, he had the oddest flash of parental feeling just then.

"Seriously," she continued, "Kristen's a nice girl."

"Seriously," Doug repeated, "I have no doubt. She's still a little young for me."

When Life Tumbles In

"OK," his sister acquiesced. "But you have my permission if you change your mind."

"Permission for what?"

"To date my friend, you big goof. I give you my blessing."

"Like I need it," he snorted, "Your Majesty."

"You know what I mean," Cat protested.

"Yeah, I do. Thanks for the good thoughts."

"And thanks for not giving Brian a hard time. I know you don't like him much."

Doug paused, then said, "I may have been wrong about him."

The comment plainly astonished her.

"All I'm saying," he continued, "is that he may be worth a second look after all." Then he flicked off the overhead light and closed the door before Cat could think of something to say. Next he made a careful sweep of the house, picking up, straightening, and cleaning. He planned on telling their parents about the party—he wasn't any good at deception—but he didn't want to apologize to them for the mess he hadn't cleaned up. After all, he was trustworthy, and so was Cat. He wanted them to know it.

15
Changing Directions

"I thought I'd go running before breakfast," Doug said. "Want to come along?"

He had taken the entire weekend off, and after the party the night before, he found himself needing a good, long run. Their parents would be back sometime in the afternoon or early evening. A morning run would do him good . . . and Cat, too, if everything worked out.

She had wanted a morning shower, but he convinced her just to wash her face and wave a comb through her hair. Anything more, he told her, and his morning run would be an afternoon one. Jason usually worked in the afternoon, though he didn't tell her that.

Doug hadn't seen him at the track during the whole past week, but there he was, easily passing the fair-weather runners. Real runners wore comfortable clothing—loose, airy stuff that allowed the sweat to do its necessary work. Jason ran in a pair of paint-stained gym shorts and an oversize T-shirt with the espresso stand's Red Cross logo front and back. He wore a Seattle Mariners ball cap pulled low over his eyes and Nikes so old the "swoosh" was chocolate-colored.

Seeing him out there, Doug said nothing, guessing that Cat had not spotted him quite yet. He parked her in the morning sun, close to the shade if she got too hot. His sister had brought a small bottle of water, a bagel to nibble, and her sketchbook. She had sunglasses and a black Seahawks ball cap to shade her eyes while she drew. Doug shed his sweatshirt and jammed his own Boeing cap on over unruly hair. Cat surprised him with a request.

"By the way, Dog, if someone should want to stop and talk to me, you don't have to run right over and scare him. OK?"

He smiled. So she'd seen him after all.

"Sure, I'll let 'em live. Promise."

Doug did a couple slow stretches, timing his entrance on the track so that it wouldn't be so obvious that he wanted Jason to catch him. He'd have to work at it. And Jason obliged, moving easily up beside him after half a lap.

"Hi."

Doug nodded back. "You asked about my sister. She's here." He tilted his head in her direction.

"I saw." Jason glanced over at him. "You mind if I talk with her?"

"I'm not her father."

"But you're the guard dog, right?"

"Right," Doug grinned in spite of himself. "She said you treated her nice in the hospital. You got my permission."

Jason nodded and smiled. "You growl really good."

"I also bite."

"I have no doubt."

The younger man dropped back to a walk while Doug picked up his pace, heading into another lap. The next time he passed, he could see them both talking. She even showed him her sketchbook. Jason had slipped on a baggy old hospital sweatshirt with the arms torn out, and he sat cross-legged on the grass next to Cat's wheelchair, going through her sketches one by one.

Although he probably could've done more, Doug called it quits after five miles, walking a lap to cool down before ambling over to the couple still talking together.

"Cat's pretty good," Jason said, tapping the sketchbook with a finger.

"Yeah, she is."

Jason turned to Cat. "How long have you been doing this?"

"Since Christmas. Seriously anyway. Doug bought me my first stuff."

"You've gotten this good in just a few months?" Jason was incredulous.

"Well, I draw a lot."

"I guess," he whistled low. "And I like your sense of humor." He pointed to her current sketch of Doug jogging, a lanky blood-

Changing Directions

hound in sweats and battered sneakers. Although her brother had seen it before, he spotted something new in the picture—a second runner with winged sandals and helmet.

"Who's the FTD florist guy?" Doug wanted to know.

"That's not the flower guy—it's Mercury, the winged messenger of the gods."

"Uh-huh."

"You know. Greek mythology. Jason. As in Jason and the golden fleece."

"Bit of a stretch there," Doug commented. "Mixing stories up, aren't you?"

"She's better at this than you are," Jason smiled wryly.

Doug shrugged, picked up his own water bottle, drank a couple swallows, then sprayed some over his head after taking his cap off.

Jason changed the subject. "How far do you run?"

"Depends on how bad the day is."

"Ah."

"What's 'ah'?"

"People run for different reasons. Most of them come out to show off their 'cool' running clothes or to scope the guys and girls. They do a couple laps, breathe hard for a while, and get that righteous feeling, you know? 'I really put in an effort today, boy!' When they're sore the next day, they never return.

"You run *from* something. The worse the day, the harder you run. The pain, the exertion, helps you bury all the other things in your life so you can function the rest of the time. There are some good runners who do just what you do. But the great ones . . . they run *for* something."

Doug's eyebrows went up, but he only grunted noncommittally. It made sense and confirmed some of his own suspicions. Cat beat him to the question he was about to ask.

"What kind of runner are you?" she asked, putting Jason on the spot.

"I run for joy," he said quite seriously.

"Joy?" Doug snorted. He couldn't remember the last time he'd felt joyous. It was the strangest thing he'd ever heard.

"When you run until you 'don't feel bad,' that's different from running until you feel good."

"I'll have to take your word for it," Doug shrugged again.

"What's your longest run?" Jason asked.

"Ten miles. Twelve once on a good day."

"Ever thought of trying a marathon?"

Doug shook his head. *Twenty-six miles and change.* It sounded like more work than he wanted to think about.

"Consider it," Jason continued. "I'm working on a project. Looking for somebody who takes it seriously."

"Running?"

Jason nodded. "Yeah. You look like it means life or death to you."

Doug had to admit the kid wasn't far off the mark there.

16

Where To From Here?

Nancy and Carter Walker returned home that afternoon looking a bit more relaxed than they had two days earlier. Doug knew that time away—time alone together—was not the complete cure to his parents' problems, but sometimes a Band-Aid was all one had.

Doug helped his father unload the car while Mom went in to use the bathroom and "hug Cat." He knew that she was making sure that his sister was all right. Everybody understood what she really meant, and though some might have taken offense, he didn't. That was the way Mom was.

Using the time alone with his father, Doug told him about the party that he'd orchestrated the night before. Once Mr. Carter had confirmed that Doug had behaved responsibly, he gave his blessing.

"You know, you could have asked before we left," his father pointed out.

"Uhmm. Then you and Mom would have worried about us, checked on us, maybe come back early . . . all for nothing. Besides, sometimes it's better to apologize for something you've done than to ask permission to do it in the first place."

"Who taught you *that?*"

"Jerry said he learned that from you."

His father chuckled. "I figured that would come back and bite me someday."

Mom wasn't nearly as forgiving, but part of that, Doug guessed, was that he'd been right about her reactions. She preferred to think of herself as prudent, when in reality she just plain worried too much. Doug's assessment didn't please her at all. But finally Cat convinced her that everything had gone well in her absence.

"You're not always going to have to take care of me, Mom."

"I don't mind taking care of you, honey," she objected.

"But *I* do," Cat surprised her. "I've got to get back into the world. I need to know I can make a difference in it, even like this."

Their mother got a little teary over that, and so did Cat. Doug managed to change the subject by asking them about their weekend, where they'd gone, what they'd done and seen.

They'd taken the scenic route south on Chuckanut Drive, following the shoreline of the bay and all its little inlets, finally crossing Deception Pass to pick up the ferry from Whidbey Island to Port Townsend. As they'd stood on the ferry deck in the failing light they had watched a pod of orcas in the distance. That first night they'd stayed at Groveland Cottage, a wonderful little bed and breakfast place north of Sequim on the Olympic Peninsula. From their bedroom window that night they could see the sweeping beam of the lighthouse out on the Dungeness Spit. Most of the next day they'd puttered about the peninsula, driving up to Hurricane Ridge and visiting the Animal Farm. Driving back later that afternoon, they'd taken an inexpensive room in tiny LaConner and finished their weekend the next day by strolling through the burgeoning tulip farms near Mt. Vernon.

"I've never seen such color!" Mom exclaimed. "Row after row of reds, yellows, whites—it was wonderful."

For some reason, when they told about how *their* weekend had gone, Cat didn't mention meeting Jason at the track that morning. Taking his cue from her, Doug said nothing as well. It was their secret, and he decided he liked that. He checked in with Cat at bedtime again.

"I had a good weekend, Dog."

"Me, too," he agreed. "Though you've been kind of quiet this evening. Did I tire you out?"

"No, just letting Mom and Dad have the spotlight for a while. And I've been remembering again . . . about the accident."

"Oh?" he said quietly, sitting on the edge of her bed.

"It was my fault." She closed her eyes.

"Why do you say that?"

"At the party, Brian returned a cassette to me, the Alanis Morisette tape I wanted to play for him on the way to pick up his cousin. When he returned it to me, he said he'd scavenged it from what was left of his car. He couldn't remember it, and he thought maybe it was mine."

Doug had been completely unaware of that little moment. He hadn't seen the exchange, hadn't noticed anything odd at all between his sister and Brian. Now he wondered what else he'd missed.

"Did you see his hand?" Cat asked.

Doug shook his head, words failing.

"Cut himself crawling into the wreck. Said he saw our blood all over the seat and the dashboard. He was so angry with himself because he couldn't remember what happened, and he was so sure it was his fault. And I was hurt, and he wasn't. But he was wrong. It was *my* fault."

Doug's heart beat louder in his chest, thrashing like an animal trying to escape a trap.

"It was raining and slick. I remember."

So did Doug. *A silver T-Bird in a wash of cold rain. The sound of caliper brakes slipping on wet bike tires.*

"I tried to put the cassette in his player, but I got it in wrong, and while I was turning it over I dropped it on the floor. Neither of us could reach it. We were wearing seat belts. I undid mine."

Cat closed her eyes, and her breath caught in the back of her throat. She forced herself to breathe.

"I reached over, scooted almost off the seat to pick it up. Brian tried to help. He must've looked away from the road for a second. Next thing I knew he was fighting the wheel, the car was making strange noises—like it was screaming—and I hit my head. Then nothing."

Closing his eyes, Doug took her hand and stroked it wordlessly.

"It was all my fault," she whispered in a tear-choked voice. *"My* fault. Not Brian's."

"Nobody's blaming you, Cat," Doug forced his voice to steady, to be strong, "or Brian either, for that matter."

"I've got to tell Brian."

"It won't change how he feels."

"But *I* caused the accident, totaled his car, and put us both in the hospital."

"I think he'd agree you've paid the price for that mistake. But you're right. You should tell him. Just don't be surprised if it doesn't make any difference. Good men pick up the slack, take responsibility for making things better. Now he has a real good reason to make things better. He'll be happy that he didn't hurt you, but he'll shoulder the blame anyway."

"Is this a guy thing?"

"It's the right thing to do," her brother insisted. "After all, he was the driver and shouldn't have let you take off your seat belt. And he should have kept his eye on the road. He made mistakes too. Maybe by understanding what really happened, he can forgive himself, accept responsibility for those mistakes, and grow up."

And maybe I can too, Doug thought. He hoped so.

"That doesn't make much sense to me."

"You need more testosterone before you'll understand that one." The corner of his mouth twitched into a smile. "You're just the sister."

"This should change things. Knowing how it happened should make a difference somehow."

"Down the road maybe. A lot of that's up to you. What do you want?"

Cat looked at him for a long time. He'd started by holding her hand. Now she was holding his.

"I guess we can both ask ourselves that question," she said finally.

Doug nodded. "I guess we can."

17

Knowing When to Run

The blustery, wet days of early spring passed, the weather gradually warming into the first days of summer. Close to the bay as the city was, summer temperatures never really climbed too high, but Doug found he could leave his coat behind more and more often. He continued running, extending his distance once in a while when he had the time and the light, just to see how far he could push himself. Ten miles became routine, with an occasional 12 miles, and once 15, though that had seemed too much too soon. He didn't repeat that.

Jason ran with him whenever their schedules crossed, which wasn't all that often until school let out for the summer. Then the younger man started working longer hours at Thirst Aid, the hospital espresso stand. During the school year he did his homework there in between customers, and according to Cat, he was a reasonably good student. But for Doug he was just pleasant company, a companionably silent running partner who could match his pace or move out on his own if need be. Soon Doug found himself hoping that Jason would be at the track when he went there to run.

They talked, after a fashion, about work, about sports, about girls, but it was to Cat that Jason opened up. And it was from her that Doug learned the young man was no stranger to tragedy. His parents had died in a car accident, and afterward he had gone to live with his older brother and his new wife. Devastated by the loss of his parents, Jason had picked up the job at the espresso stand as a form of grief therapy. But it was his brother's young wife who'd suggested giving a flower to a patient who'd survived the very thing that had killed his mother and father.

That act became Jason's memorial to them, that flower becoming two, then six, then dozens, given singly, anonymously, with the hope of full recovery. Anonymous, at least, until one of those patients had actually asked where the flower had come from. Which was how Jason had met Cat all those months ago. And why they were now friends.

One summer evening, early in June, Doug came to the end of a run and discovered a friend of his own waiting patiently for him to finish. More than a friend, actually . . . and less.

"Hello," Jill said, brushing a strand of red hair behind her ear, just as he remembered.

"Hello," he replied, picking up the towel he'd left hanging on the bleachers and draping it around his neck.

"School's out," she said by way of explanation.

"H'mmm," Doug nodded, agreeable enough, he thought. Funny that he hadn't kept track of that. But it hadn't seemed all that important.

"Can I talk with you?"

"Walk with me," he replied. "I need to cool down."

Doug didn't like surprises. The last few hadn't been much fun, and he didn't have time in his life for even a little bit more chaos right now. He could have kicked himself for not expecting something like this. Sooner or later it was inevitable that their paths would cross. They had the same former classmates, attended the same church, and were both addicted to pistachio-almond ice cream. Although he had known that, he just hadn't expected Jill to come looking for him.

Every joint in his body felt loose, as if he were held together by rubber bands. Normally it was a wonderful feeling, but he didn't want to be too relaxed right now. He needed to be sharp here, not fluid, though he didn't think he had any edge to himself. Perhaps it was safer that way.

"I didn't know you ran."

"Started after Christmas," he explained, dabbing his face with the towel and wondering if she'd understand why the timing was significant.

"You run a long time—that's impressive."

Knowing When to Run

"I find it . . . helpful," he said, trying to keep it vague.

"You didn't write back to me."

"H'mmm?"

"After I wrote to you about Scott, you didn't write back."

"Scott? That's his name, huh?"

Suddenly Doug felt like running, tired as he was. He had to physically throttle back to keep from breaking into a run, though he did pick up his walking pace. Just a bit. Jill matched it, uncomfortable, but unsure why.

"Why didn't you write?" she asked again.

"I didn't see the point."

"The point?" She seemed surprised.

"Was it going to change your mind?"

Feeling the anger blossom down deep and begin to push aside the fatigue, he wanted to slip into an easy, loping jog. Though he kept a firm grip on his body, his mind began to run.

"My point was to talk about how you felt!"

"What's the point in *that*? You met someone else and chose him, not me. Why would you be worried about how *I* felt?"

In his mind he was running flat out, arms and legs pumping, the wind in his face.

"Because you're my friend," she said simply.

Now he *had* to run. If he didn't do it now he was going to explode . . . maybe hurt someone—he now discovered to his surprise—that he still cared about. She touched his arm, not knowing how out of control he was, slowed his lengthening stride.

"You'd do that to a friend?" he turned on her. He had trouble believing it.

"I know you're angry—" she began.

"Yes," he said, "and hurt and lonely. That's about all there is left, but I haven't died from it. Maybe I'll grow out of it. But not right now, I think."

Jill didn't have anything to say. Just a funny look on her face, as if she'd been practicing this conversation for days, and it hadn't gone quite the way that she'd planned.

"I can't be your friend right now," he said, wanting no misunderstanding. "I don't want to be."

Only when he turned and walked away did he discover that he didn't feel like running anymore. And he hadn't exploded. He'd told Jill the truth . . . about how he *felt!*

That surprised him more than he could say.

18
Surprises

Just full of surprises, Doug thought. *I hate surprises.*

The first one had come from Mom as he was leaving for work.

"Douglas, make sure you're home for dinner by 6:00. All right?"

"My shift ends around 3:00," he replied, knotting his tie as he went out the front door. "Shouldn't be a problem." Then he paused and looked back through the screen door. "What's up?"

"We have a dinner guest. Your running friend Jason is coming over. He has something he wants to talk to us about."

"Jason? I didn't even know you knew him."

"Douglas, I'd have to have been deaf and blind not to know him. Your sister talks about him all the time. Once in a while he stops by to check on her and brings a flower for her each time. I'm afraid your sister is quite smitten."

Smitten? Doug wondered. Mom actually *used* that word? Wasn't that how they talked in the Bible? Or was that Shakespeare? Only Mom could pull that off with a straight face. So . . . Jason was coming for dinner. That was worth thinking about, so he did, all the way to work, where Brent caught him at the door with the next surprise.

"Walker! Got a job for you."

"Sure," Doug said.

"Meet Kristen. New kid on the block."

"Hi, Dog," she said with a wry smile. "Cat said you were looking for summer help."

"You two know each other?" Brent asked.

"My sister and Kristen are friends."

"Peachy," Brent smirked. "She's on register three today. In between customers, teach her how to face. Start over in OTC."

"OK."

Then Brent and his ever-present clipboard disappeared around the corner of a display.

"Is it just me," Kristen wondered, "or did somebody drop him on his head when he was a baby?"

Doug stifled a laugh. "No. Your instincts are good."

"What's oh-tee-cee?"

"Over-the-counter drugs," he explained. "Lots of little bottles to knock over. Job security," he added.

She smiled at him, and Doug liked it.

Surprise, surprise.

But the biggest surprise came that evening when Jason drove up to the curb in front of the house in his brother's pick-up truck. Cat wheeled herself out to meet him. Jason had to slam the truck door hard to make it stay closed, then he bent over, giving Cat a quick kiss and a hug. From behind his back he produced a flower—a single, white rosebud.

"Close your mouth, Douglas," his mother whispered in his ear.

"When did *that* happen?"

"Like all things," Mom replied, "a little at a time. You helped, you know. He said you'd given your permission." She smiled.

"To *talk* to her," Doug muttered.

"Apparently," she chuckled, "he talks very well."

Cat had cooked chili and made grilled cheese sandwiches for dinner that night. She'd diced green, orange, yellow, and red peppers to add to the three kinds of beans and sautéed Walla Walla Sweet onions. For bite, she'd swirled in bits of jalapeño, and everybody but Mom had seconds.

Their father had even made a point of being home to meet Jason, but as far as Doug could tell, the young man wasn't intimidated in the least. By the end of the meal it seemed quite normal to have him there at the table with the rest of the family.

"Cat tells me you have an idea you wanted to talk with us about," Mr. Carter prompted, carrying empty bowls to the sink.

"Yes, sir," Jason began. "I wanted to talk to you all, because to one extent or another, you'll all be involved."

Dessert was a common bowl filled with sliced apples, orange wedges, grapes, and melon balls. Jason forked an orange, but didn't eat it immediately.

Surprises

"Next fall the hospital will conduct its annual fund-raising campaign. This year's project involves up-grading the pediatrics wing. One of the ideas the board has OKed is to host a marathon through the streets of town. Participants will raise money by getting sponsors to pay by the mile."

"I know where this is going," Doug muttered as he crunched an apple slice.

"Huh?" Jason glanced over at him.

"You want me to run the marathon with you, right?"

"Not exactly. I'm going to be too busy helping with support services such as getting water to all the sites along the route. I'd like to run, but I won't have time."

"Then you want me to run alone?"

"Actually," Cat broke in, *"I'm* going to enter the marathon. I need you as a teammate."

Doug had no idea what to say. His father didn't have that problem.

"I realize that wheelchair athletes compete in marathons all the time, and Cat's made remarkable progress, but she's not in shape to push a wheelchair for 26 miles. It hasn't even been a year since the accident."

Mom hadn't said a word yet, which Doug found odd, until he realized that this idea hadn't been a surprise to her. She'd heard all this before. Jason and Cat had run it past her already . . . *and gotten her blessing!* At least enough agreement to present it to the rest of the family.

"We thought of that," Cat interjected, back in the conversation, her excitement growing as he talked. "Jason's brother has agreed to help me train, build my upper body strength and stamina. That gives me four months or so to get ready."

"Still, we don't expect Cat to be able to do it alone," Jason said. "That's why we need you, Dog. You'll run with her, and I'll be the coach. It'll be a team effort."

Doug wasn't convinced. "I'm not sure *I* can even run a marathon."

"Won't be easy," Jason agreed. "You and Cat will have to train all summer just to get ready. But the biggest problem is her chair. It's way too heavy for racing."

"But we worked out a solution to that problem," Cat grinned.

"Let me show you." Jason got up from the table.

Leading the family outside to his pickup parked at the curb, he pulled back a tarp covering something mechanical in the bed. Then reaching in, he lifted out a wheelchair so light he needed to use only one hand.

"One of the specialists my brother works with builds custom-made wheelchairs and donated this. He called it"—Jason breathed in near reverence—"the Machine! Lightweight, tough, and even more stable than regular chairs."

Doug thought it looked like something from a science fiction movie. The titanium frame and graphite-rimmed wheels were incredibly strong for their weight. The wheels leaned in for stability, and the seat was triple-stitched blue nylon. The Machine gleamed in the light of the fading sun. It was low, fast, and maneuverable. Cat couldn't wait to try it out.

Jason gifted her with a pair of racing gloves, their palms double thick to protect her hands from wheel burn. Then he helped her transfer from her chair into the racing sling of the Machine. While she tried it out on the sidewalk, Jason showed them the push bar that would attach to the frame so Doug could assist when Cat got tired. Doug took him aside.

"What are you thinking?" he whispered hoarsely. "What if I don't have it in me to do this?"

"I think you do. You've always needed something to run for, and now you've got it. Run for Cat."

"For Cat?"

"She needs you, Dog. You're right. She can't do it without you, and without her, neither can you. You need each other. If it helps at all, we've even got sponsors."

"What!"

"Yeah!" Jason grinned. "The Therapy Department is tossing in a hundred bucks each for the right to put the department logo on your T-shirts. Between the physical therapists and the occupational therapists, that's $500 for the hospital without even taking a step. Cat's agreed to work as a fund-raiser, and your mother will help her with that. Maybe your father can swing a corporate donation, too."

"Jason, we can't win!"

"Who said 'win'?" Jason clapped a hand on Doug's shoulder. "All you have to do is *finish*. Can you *walk* 26 miles?"

"I don't know." Doug shook his head, but he felt swept along in spite of himself. "I guess we'll find out."

19

The Whole Truth, and Nothing But

That summer Doug wore out a pair of running shoes, then bought and thoroughly broke in another. He ran alone, he ran with Jason, and he ran pushing Cat's regular wheelchair while she practiced in the Machine. And from time to time Cat submitted to being pushed about so that Doug could get a feeling for running with her.

As it turned out, the therapists had sort of adopted them, welcoming them into an extended professional family, and they found themselves children of a whole village of mothers and fathers. The therapists were more than willing to teach Cat and Doug what they needed to know. From the sports trainers who contracted with the hospital, the brother and sister learned about taping toes and ankles, about healing blisters and preventing shin splints. Doug discovered the principles of carbo-loading from the hospital dietitian and how to breathe properly from Jean's husband, who turned out to be a black belt. But more important, he experienced what it was like to be part of a team in which every decision affected everyone else.

Jason took his role as coach seriously, seeing to it that both he and Cat worked out in the hospital weight room on a regular basis. Surprisingly, it was there instead of the track that Doug began to face some of the truths in his life. While running he could vanish into the rhythm of his body. But lifting weights was another matter entirely. Time was built in between sets for rest, for setting up the next exercise, and for stretching. He found there was nothing left but to look himself straight in the eye reflected in the wall mirrors and raise tough questions. Even so, it wasn't always him doing the asking.

"What's it like," Cat wanted to know one day, "losing your parents?"

The Whole Truth, and Nothing But

Doug was finishing his second set at 95 pounds on one of the Nautilus machines designed to work the muscles on the inside and outside of the thighs. Sweat trickled into the small of his back, and though his muscles were "talking to him," he hadn't missed her question.

She was resting between sets of her own, working under Jason's watchful eye, building her upper body strength. Jason tossed her a towel that she used to dab delicately at her face. He didn't answer right away.

"I don't know," he shrugged. "What's it like to lose the use of your legs?" he asked in return. "Or the girl you thought loved you?" He glanced over at Doug. "I can describe it, I guess, but understanding it?"

The weight room was empty except for the three of them. On a hot summer day nobody would be inside working out if they didn't have to be, even if the place *was* air-conditioned. There was nobody nearby to overhear, no one wanting to use the equipment. The only sound of activity came from the pool down the hall where a therapist was working with a patient.

"They were the center of my world," Jason admitted. "Most of what I knew about life, I learned from them. I got my picture of God from them, watching them. When they were gone"—he ran his hand through damp hair—"my world lost its foundation. My brother took me into his family, saved my life. But it was a long time before I believed in God again. If my parents could die like that, He couldn't be much of a God."

"Now *that* I understand," Doug said. "How can God stand by and let this happen? He's either not as all-powerful as everybody thinks, or He's not as loving. Either way we lose."

Cat was completely silent. Although Doug had never expressed his feeling before, he could see a look of agreement in her eyes.

"Now I know why you run," Jason sighed. He pressed his hands against his face as if he were holding something inside from escaping. "Let me tell you what I think," he said finally. "I have no facts to support this and no way to prove it. It's just something I've come to believe. I think that there is something Cat's been given to do, some great thing that she can accomplish only sitting in her wheelchair."

Jason walked away a couple steps, his back to them both. He stood there stiffly, not seeming to know what to do with his hands. Cat stared at the wall—at something only she could see. Doug wasn't sure, but he thought he saw the glimmer of tears in the corner of her eye.

"I read a story once," Jason turned around, "about a man who believed if he could just tie himself up correctly, he could fly."

"*That* is truly crazed," Doug interrupted. "Let me tell you what *I* think. You gotta be careful what you ask God for, 'cause you might just get it. When Cat was hurt I prayed that God wouldn't let her die. I just forgot to ask about the 'disabled' part."

"Dog!" Jason exclaimed almost in disbelief. "You talk as if God was some kind of cosmic genie! You don't have to speak the right words or dance around an altar or be a good enough person for Him to care about you. God always gives you His best. It's just we can't always see it . . . or understand it when we do see it."

Doug wished that were true—he really did. He was carrying so much emotional weight around. If he once laid it down, he didn't think he'd ever have enough strength to pick it back up again. Cat must have read his mind.

"It's not your fault, Dog," she said with a sniffle. "Let it go. Time to . . . move on."

Her brother slammed the weight key up five more pounds, and with a groan forced his legs together against the machine's 100 pounds of resistance.

"I'm trying!" he muttered between clenched teeth. *I'm really trying!*

20

On the Road to Damascus

Oddly enough, it was the smell of frying onions that convinced Doug that something real in his life had changed for the better. He didn't know what that something was . . . . or when exactly it had happened. But the first time he'd stepped onto the midway of the Whatcom County Fair he'd realized he was happy. No blinding light. No gentle voice from the sky asking questions. And the asphalt pavement between booths selling ice cream, cotton candy, corn on the cob, elephant ears, caramel apples, and onion rings bore no resemblance to the road to Damascus. But there it was—something was different.

Maybe he just wasn't as angry at the world and at God as he'd been the day before. Being angry all the time was hard work, after all, and Doug could maintain only a slow burn in the pit of his stomach *most,* but not all, of the time. But happiness? Occasional spikes of pleasant feeling from time to time, maybe, returning to normal levels of irritation soon after. But this was better, lasted longer, and seemed without cause. He had no idea what had prompted it, but feeling happy once in a while felt pretty good.

Cat had volunteered to help at the hospital's booth at the fair, handing out information and signing up sponsors for the marathon. Their mother brought her out each morning, made certain she was well looked after by fellow volunteers, then left for some well-deserved time for herself. Doug always stopped by after work to pick her up and bring her home.

As designated transport for his sister, he got into the fairgrounds for free, and he took advantage of it. He got to know Blumbo the Clown, who worked the entry gates on the fair's behalf, blowing up balloon animals and performing simple magic tricks. And he sampled the food.

If one listened to the media, fair food was fattening, poorly prepared, and occasionally dangerous. But it also tasted wonderful! Corn on the cob dripping with butter and sprinkled with salt. Baked potatoes with a hundred different toppings from chili to broccoli and cheese. Sno-cones with sugared syrups flavoring their cores. Fresh scones with strawberry jam.

Also he visited the animals, especially the horses, fleet and powerful, their muzzles against the walls of their stalls as they munched hay. They ranged from the ponies that pulled wagons in "eight-up" competitions to the massive Percherons, whose muscled hindquarters seemed to tower over his head. Cows, pigs, sheep, and goats filled other stalls. The only place he didn't visit housed the poultry. The feathers always made him sneeze.

The outdoor stages boasted country singers and belly dancers, karate students and hypnotists. The wildly lit carnival rides didn't interest him as much for their sensations as for their color and sound, though he did like the bumper cars. Still, since Cat's accident they'd lost their attraction somewhat.

Inside the commercial exhibit building Cat was talking earnestly with a man in casual but expensive clothing. Doug hung back and watched as the man nodded a couple times, took the pen Cat offered, and signed the sponsor sheet. After the individual had gone, Doug sauntered over.

"You know who that was?" she asked excitedly.

Her brother shook his head.

"An executive for the Cordman Foundation!" she beamed. "He gave me a $1,000 personal pledge, whether we cross the finish line or not!"

She was good at this, Doug had to give her credit. On her own, Cat had been contacting businesses all over the county, arranging appointments to talk about supporting the hospital's fund-raising campaign. Sometimes all she got for her trouble was "thank you, but not this year." Most of the time, though, she received some kind of pledge, because, as she delicately put it, "It's hard to turn down a little crippled girl who's asking for money for someone else." Occasionally she lucked out.

"What's the grand total so far?"

"Thirty-six thousand four hundred ninety-two dollars if we finish the race!"

"Keeping close account, are we?" Doug chuckled. "You about ready to call it a day?"

Cat nodded, said goodbye to her coworkers, and wheeled herself out of the booth. The muscles in her arms and shoulders testified to the hours of upper body training she'd been doing the past months.

"Got a couple stops to make," she said as they left the building. "The artwork was judged today. I want to see if I won anything. And then I want to stop for some onion rings."

Doug smiled, but kept it to himself. He knew what Cat was planning. Kristen worked an evening stint at the kiosk serving onion rings—he'd already made a point of finding out. Cat wanted to fix him up with her friend without being too terribly obvious about it, which he found rather endearing. Somehow he kind of hoped it would all work out.

A slow trickle of people meandered along the aisles of the arts and crafts exhibit building. This year's theme was "Perspective," and Cat had responded to the idea by creating a series of four pen and ink sketches hung in a spiral. Each drawing was larger than the next, even though each one dealt with a smaller and smaller subject. The first sketch was a pastoral: a farmhouse, pasture, and grazing horse as seen from a nearby hilltop. The second picture zoomed in on the same scene, relegating the farmhouse to a slash of ink at the side of the piece and focusing on the horse behind its fence. The third looked down at the grazing horse's back, a mushroom spreading nearby. The fourth and final sketch was a ground-level close-up of the mushroom, the horse's muzzle off to one side, and in the distance, past the farmhouse and fencepost, a careful observer would note a tiny figure on a hilltop in a wheelchair.

Entitled "Another Way of Looking," the series of drawings impressed Doug, but then anything Cat drew he liked. He was, perhaps, not the best judge. His sister impatiently hurried over to the display and didn't hide her disappointment that the series had no little ribbons hanging nearby.

"How do they judge stuff like this?" Doug asked.

He'd seen the painting that had taken first place, and he wondered how anyone would even know whether it was hung right side up.

"Apparently," she snapped, "I'm the wrong person to ask."

"What about your other entry?"

At Doug's urging, Cat had reworked the drawing she'd made of him during his bout with the flu last winter. Entered under the category of "Whimsy," the sketch was called "Sick as a Dog" and was a particular favorite of his. She'd added considerable detail, and though there was no prize ribbon hanging from this one either, it had a sign marked "Sold."

"Sold?" Doug asked. "Can they do that?"

Cat nodded. "I gave them permission to sell it for $25 dollars if someone really wanted it."

"Someone bought it!" Doug smiled.

"I wonder who . . ." Her voice trailed off; then she was gone. When she returned, she was smiling.

"Where'd you go?"

"I went to check the registry to see who bought it."

"And?"

"Kristen."

"Kristen?"

"H'mm. Guess why."

"She knows good work when she sees it?"

Cat made an exasperated sound. "Kristen bought it because it's a picture of you."

"Oh. I guess that's not so bad either."

"Come on. Let's go get some onion rings."

That sounded good to him.

21

One Foot in Front of the Other

Running had become prayer for Doug. Not the cowering, shoulder-hunched, neck-bowed, defeated prayer of the victim, but the exuberant, heart-pumping, song-singing prayer of those who'd gone down into the valley and were surprised to be coming out of it. He set himself in motion and opened his soul. At last he understood what Jason had meant about running for the joy of it.

While it was true that he never spotted angels keeping pace with him as he practiced pushing Cat's modified wheelchair about the neighborhood, he didn't think he was ever really alone either. Jason's own faith, held in the face of his own pain, had shown Doug that such a life was possible. Not easy, but possible.

A local radio station, KGMI-KISM, had heard about them. Jason had never admitted to it, but Doug was certain he'd had a hand in it. One of the deejays was so taken with them that he offered to do not only an interview but also weekly updates until the race. That original interview had caught the attention of a reporter at the Bellingham *Herald* who wrote a feature for the Sunday edition on the "Cat and Dog Racing Team," as they'd come to be called. They'd even gotten a 10-second flash during a quick interview about the hospital's fund-raising campaign on KVOS-TV.

All the pieces were coming together, generating a momentum that neither he nor Cat had anticipated. With Cat pushing for more donors every day and Kristen trying ever-crazier ideas to raise money, Doug found himself on the receiving end of near-celebrity status. He'd only just managed to convince Kristen that shaving her head to raise money was a terrible waste of beautiful black hair. She'd cut a snip, bound it in a lacy ribbon, and given it to him. Touched by the gesture, he had kissed her on the cheek. She had blushed hugely.

The employees at the store, under Kristen's direction, had

formed two- and three-person cheering squads, who vowed to post themselves throughout the race to provide them with moral support. Doug's father had secured a $1,000 corporate gift for the hospital based on all the positive press his son had brought to the store just by working there.

Finally Doug had even called Jill, just to let her know that he'd changed his mind, that they could indeed be friends. But their paths didn't cross much anymore, and he didn't feel his heart clench at the mere sight of her.

"Just wanted you to know," he'd said over the phone, "that I'm calmer these days."

"I'm sorry it's so awkward," she answered.

"Well, maybe that'll pass, too."

They had a history, he and Jill. Just no future that he could foresee. They'd finally taken leave of each other with no one in pain.

"Why wait 20 years to make up," he said. "That'd be stupid."

Even so, Doug recognized that he would always know in his heart where Jill was.

The night before the race Doug slept fitfully. Weather reports were mixed, calling for early morning clouds and possible light drizzle with some clearing for later in the day. He knew it would be better if things stayed somewhat cool, but the morning clouds seemed ominous.

Cat had slept no better, she admitted, spending her wakeful time going over the race route in her mind. She'd finally gotten up early, meticulously cleaning up and checking the Machine and their gear. Neither of them could eat. They managed only to sip glasses of fruit juice, which set no better on nervous stomachs.

Jason had come over the night before with their "uniforms": loose sweats over running shorts in the hospital's colors, blue and white; big, baggy T-shirts emblazoned front and back with the Therapy Department's logo, a flying kite, its tail formed from the words "Skills for the Job of Living." They even had the Red Cross coffee cup logo from Jason's espresso bar Thirst Aid sewn as a patch on their right shoulders. Their father had given them Sharpe's Drugs baseball caps. Doug felt like a billboard in motion, but he kept his feelings to himself.

Their parents drove them down to Civic Field, the starting point and finish line of the race. Dad folded out the Machine, helped transfer Cat to it, and threaded her catheter line back to the collector in the chair's backpack. Doug fitted the custom push rails into place with a solid "click." Mom insisted on slathering sunscreen on everyone and hugged them both.

"We just wanted you to know," their father said in a tight voice, "your mother and I are proud of you. Just . . ."—his words failed—". . . proud of you."

Mom and Dad promised to meet them at the finish line, whenever they came in, then they withdrew when Jason appeared to escort them to the staging area for the participants. Competitors filled the place, and Cat wasn't the only disabled athlete. There were three other wheelchair contestants from around the region and an amputee running on a prosthetic leg. Each of the wheelchair athletes, including a woman from a neighboring county, introduced themselves, traded stories, and wished them well. Doug and his sister were the only team and the only rookies participating with the disabled.

"OK"—Jason rubbed his hands together—"remember our strategy. We're not out to beat anybody, so we don't have to worry about anybody's pace but our own. Don't go out fast even though you'll want to. The crowd just sort of overwhelms you with the urge to do it, but you have to resist. You won't have anything left to finish with if you use it up too early."

"Right," Cat jumped in. "I have the stopwatch. We're shooting for about 12-minute miles."

"Exactly," Jason nodded. "A good, solid run would bring you in under three hours, but you guys can't hope to match that pace. I'm guessing more like five or six hours. Don't forget to drink. There will be stations all along the route with water and juice to keep you hydrated. You can collapse from dehydration as fast as fatigue."

When Life Tumbles In

"Yeah, yeah, we got it," Doug growled.

"I'll be all along the route. Sometimes you'll see me, and sometimes you won't, but I'll be close no matter what."

Then Jason ran a nervous hand through his hair.

"Would it be OK if I prayed with you before it all starts?"

Cat smiled the purest smile just then, Doug thought. If he hadn't known better, he'd have thought she was an angel.

"Sure, Jase," Doug spoke for them both.

As Cat bent forward in her chair, Doug crouched beside her, and—on one knee—Jason put his hands on both of their shoulders.

"Father God, these are my two best friends in all the world. Keep them safe, make them strong, and show them the way home. Amen."

Cat stuck out her hand, palm down and grinned. "One for all."

Doug put his hand on hers. "And all for one," he added.

Jason covered their hands with his own. "Let's rock and roll!" he shouted.

Then he produced a daisy and slipped it behind Cat's ear. "For luck," he whispered, and hugged her.

Kristen appeared out of nowhere. She hugged Cat, too, before turning to Doug. "I have something for you," she said. "Can I give it to you?"

He nodded dumbly, and she kissed him soundly on the mouth, standing on tiptoe to do it. Giggling afterwards, she slipped off into the crowd. He touched his fingers lightly to his lips.

"I think she likes you," his sister chuckled.

"Ya think?" Doug muttered back.

"Runners!" the loudspeaker blared suddenly. *"To your marks!"*

They had no more time for thought. Now it was time to do something. Something wonderful.

The start of the marathon was unlike any race Doug had ever witnessed. Nobody "toed" their marks for a fast break as sprinters did. In fact, they mostly just milled about the starting line, waiting for the gun. The mayor and the hospital's chief administrator gave short speeches thanking everyone for their hard work and the benefit the hospital would receive. Then, wisely, they got out of the way.

When the starting gun went off and the front ranks spilled across the line, Doug wanted to jump out of his skin. They were so far back in the pack that it took several seconds for enough space to clear for them to even approach the starting line.

Bicyclists, riding their own route, went out first to avoid interfering with the marathon runners. Then the runners broke out, followed by the disabled racers positioned at the back of the crowd. Cat and Doug were among the last to clear the first lap and exit Civic Field, heading up Orleans, the short entry lane that emptied out onto Lakeway Drive. Even so, Cat called back to him, "Pull back. We're going out too fast."

Doug eased back on command. Once out on Lakeway, she took over and Doug quit pushing. Cat settled into a familiar rhythm: push, glide, push, glide. Doug jogged along beside her within easy reach, finding his own accustomed pace. He felt his heart lift, the nervous tension skimming away as they set out together.

From Lakeway they turned left, passing the hospital on their right and KVOS-TV just a block later before starting down "fast food row" on Samish Way. People crowded the sidewalks the first few miles, hooting for their friends, shouting encouragement, but Doug barely heard them.

The temptation to race ahead was almost overwhelming, but he knew better than to give into it. Cat had slowed them down again after they'd been swept along through the first mile. At mileposts 2 and 3 they came in right on the mark. They'd found their pace at last.

Jason had shown up at the first mile station, Kristen at the second, then Jason again at the third near Burger King. Doug realized they were leap-frogging each other by some private arrangement. At the third mile checkpoint Doug snagged a cup of water, slammed it back, and dropped the cup in the trash can at the station's end. From Samish Way they left the main road and picked

When Life Tumbles In

up first Thirty-sixth Street, then Fielding as they wove their way through apartment buildings headed for their next long stretch of road. On Fairhaven Parkway, a road that paralleled the interstate southbound, Cat picked up a cup of Gatorade and let Doug push while she sipped quickly.

The weather, already cool, turned actually brisk, and Doug felt a few scattered drops of rain, but it never really got wet. As long as it didn't become any colder, it was good running weather. At the fifth mile they jogged past one poor runner sitting alongside the route and throwing up, a paramedic crouched next to the man. Doug hoped that wasn't an omen.

Turning right on Twelfth Street, they followed the meandering road that led into Old Fairhaven, a suburb of Bellingham, counting off miles 6, 7, and 8 in calm monotony. Cat routinely checked their times and nodded for his benefit. They could talk to each other at this pace if necessary, but conversation was uncomfortable.

Right again brought them on to Finnegan Way, plunging through the heart of the Fairhaven business district. Police rerouted traffic until all the runners had passed. Jerry appeared on the edge of the crowd out in front of the Fairhaven Library. He raised a fist and shouted, "Dog! You the Man! Go, big guy!"

Doug grinned so hard his face hurt. He waved sketchily back, slamming down another water at mile nine. At the tenth mile members of their church performed "the Wave" as he and Cat went by. His sister opted to rest for the next mile, and she began rotating her shoulder as if it hurt.

"S'up?" Doug asked.

"Cramp."

She'd done the best she could, Doug thought. They'd never believed that she'd actually be able to wheel the entire race. Ten miles was more than they could have hoped for.

"Rest," he said, gripping the push bar.

Cat nodded gratefully, but she continued to rotate the shoulder, trying to massage out the cramp.

Leaving Fairhaven behind, Doug pushed her onto Boulevard

One Foot in Front of the Other

Parkway, which skirted the harbor's edge. Though more exposed to the weather here, they noticed that the drizzle that had threatened the last couple of miles had begun to break up. The sky cleared a little bit at a time. Doug gulped down water at every station now, but he couldn't seem to get enough.

His mouth was dry, even though he tried to control his breathing through his nose. But he couldn't get enough air that way, and when he breathed through his mouth, it dried him out. It was a vicious circle. His shirt was soaked, front and back, but so far he felt that he was doing all right. Miles 11, 12, and 13 went by in a growing haze.

At the halfway point on State Street, as they headed back into downtown Bellingham, Kristen showed up on the sidelines with a cheering section from the store. He nodded at them as he and Cat swept by, shouts of "Dog! Dog! Dog!" following them. Although his sister had returned to pushing again for short stretches, her rest periods were getting longer. She wasn't going to last. Cat helped with the uphill stretches, which Doug appreciated more than he could say. By her count, they'd dropped off the pace a bit, but not seriously.

Near the fourteenth mile marker, still pounding down State Street, Doug saw Brent standing alongside the route, two little girls in his arms, a woman by his side, clapping and pointing them out to the children. Doug had never thought that Brent might have children, or that he could be married. He guessed there were lots of things he didn't know.

Cat and Doug were passing stragglers now, people who'd exhausted themselves early on and had nothing left. A woman lay in the grass on her back at curbside, taking oxygen. Two paramedics hovered over her. Doug had never gone beyond the 15-mile limit before, and when they did, he felt a surge of pleasure. He remembered Jason's comment months earlier about running to feel good instead of running to stop feeling bad. Maybe this was what he'd meant. At mileposts 16 and 17 they were back on the pace.

His legs seemed to move without any conscious effort. He

wasn't sure he could stop them, even if he tried. Feeling as if he didn't have much in common with his body, he guessed it was a fatigue stage he was going through. Stopping would take more energy than continuing on, so he kept on running.

Cat reminded him to drink, and he was surprised that he'd forgotten. It was not a good sign. As they left the downtown area behind, beginning a large loop through residential areas along James and Illinois Streets, she kept glancing back to check up on him, looking worried. He could hear nothing but his breath, his heart pumping, the pavement under his feet as he jogged along. Miles fell beneath him and beneath the wheels of her Machine.

It was somewhere along Cornwall Avenue, between mileposts 20 and 21, that he failed to see the pothole. He felt his entire left leg buckle, but he held onto the push bar and recovered quickly, grunting from the pain in his ankle.

"Doug, what happened?"

"Jammed . . . my leg . . . in a hole."

"Bad?"

"Enough. Hurts."

"Then that's it."

"Just a few more miles to go," he objected. "I can make it. *I can!*" he insisted between breaths.

Various media people had stretched out all along the route, mostly photographers sent to snap a couple rolls of film, hoping to get one or two good photos out of the lot. They were mostly interested in the front runners, though one of them in particular seemed to turn up often enough for Doug to guess he was following them. The front runners had passed the finish line a couple hours ago.

Hours? he wondered. *Have we been running that long?*

"Running" was, perhaps, not the most accurate word for what he was doing. The ankle injury had thrown off his rhythm. It was no longer a clean, slow cycling of legs and feet. He was hitching along, throwing most of his weight onto his good leg. His ankle had stopped hurting after several hundred yards, subsiding to a dull ache. Still, he didn't trust it, and he slowed to a hard walking pace.

Since his injury, Cat had tried to pick up the slack, and he was leaning heavily on the push bar to take the pressure off his leg. But she was exhausted, whimpering softly to herself when she thought he couldn't hear.

Doug wondered what they looked like to the people along the race route, to that photographer following them. Did they see the pain in their eyes? Did they ask themselves what was so important that they'd subject themselves to this ordeal? Were they crazy, after all? He couldn't have answered them. Still, he'd promised Cat he'd go the distance if he possibly could. They'd prove to everybody . . . what? What were they trying to prove?

That they were down, but not out. That there was something, some great work for them to accomplish, something only they could do, and this was the first step.

"Dear God," Doug whispered through gritted teeth, "don't let me screw up here."

But when he looked up, his heart sank. For just a moment he was certain that God had left them. Ahead at the end of the street was something Jason had warned them about.

The wall.

22

The Wall

There it was. The wall.

It was called Ellis Street, but it was really the wall.

His mind freewheeled, thought passing by in a blur while his body went on and on, pushing Cat in the Machine. Ellis ran north and south and straight up and straight down.

Whoever had plotted the race to finish up just beyond Ellis had to have known what would happen here—24 miles into a 26-mile run only to face a half-mile stretch of four-lane asphalt that gained altitude faster than a jetliner. Doug looked at it from a hundred yards out and he knew he didn't have it in him.

Jason had warned them about *the wall*. Every runner faced something like this sooner or later in the long runs. It didn't have to be a hill—that just made it worse. And his left ankle was beyond stiff. If he was lucky, maybe there'd be an earthquake and the whole street would just fall on them. Anything so he wouldn't have to climb that hill.

He and Cat had worked out a private signal. If he ever got to a point where he thought he could not go on, he was to reach up and put his hand on her shoulder. Then she would make the final decision. They both knew, and Jason agreed, that Doug would be in no condition at that point to make rational decisions. Every step of the way since he'd wrenched his ankle in that pothole he'd been praying that he'd be able to gut it out. But this? He just couldn't do it.

Doug reached a trembling hand from the Machine's push bar and set it on his sister's shoulder. She twisted around and looked into his eyes. He could see in the lines of fatigue around her eyes and mouth, the way the skin seemed pulled tight across her cheekbones, that she was as tired as he was.

"Cat," he gasped.

It was all he could get out. Looking at him, she nodded.

The Wall

And began to sing.

"'Amazing grace, how sweet the sound . . . ,'" her voice piped out, cracking, then gaining strength as she kept on.

His favorite church song.

A shudder went through him as they reached the base of the hill, and he continued to push. He couldn't run that hill or even jog it. But maybe he could walk it.

"'. . . that saved a wretch like me . . . ,'" she sang bravely, wavering in and out of tune.

The crowd that had lined the route in the early miles had thinned down to nothing, but as they'd come closer to the finish line, it began to return. The people on the sidelines stood dead still, watching them, listening to Cat. Doug put one foot in front of the other, closed his eyes, and focused on his sister's voice as well, letting the song carry them forward. Cat helped as much as she could, pushing the wheels with stiff, gloved hands, ready to throw on the brakes if he faltered so that her chair would not roll backwards. But Doug knew she was on the ragged edge, too. Where was she getting the strength to sing?

She ran through all three verses he knew, and then something special happened. A verse all their own.

"'When we have run our earthly race, beneath these stormy skies'"—she sang to him—"'then God will call us home to Him, where no one ever dies.'"

Doug could hear the tears in her voice and feel them running down his own face. He didn't have the strength to wipe them away.

"Turn, Dog," she said.

"Huh?"

"Turn," she repeated. "Turn left. We're at the top of the hill."

And they were. The Wall had come crashing down. Jericho fallen to a female Joshua in a wheelchair.

"OK," he gasped, lungs heaving, darkness creeping into the corners of his eyes.

"One more mile to go now."

Walking was all he had left now. He could look up Lakeway, past the Fred Meyers and through the intersection, and see the entrance to Civic Field. The people lining the last mile and waiting for them seemed to know what he and Cat were going through. Some shouted encouragement, others just called their names. Mostly, though, they just clapped. And as he and Cat limped by, they flowed out off the curbs and into the street behind them, following and clapping.

Doug was in real pain. The left ankle was so stiff it wouldn't flex at all. Favoring that leg for the past few miles had put more stress on his good right one, and he knew it was going south because he couldn't feel the pavement beneath his feet anymore. And he couldn't get enough air, couldn't breathe deeply enough.

Without warning, his right leg betrayed him. It just wasn't there when he threw his weight back off the stiff leg. As he flailed he lost his grip on the push bar of Cat's Machine. He went down hard on the pavement just short of the entrance to the track where the finish line awaited them. His elbow cracked on the asphalt.

Somebody touched him, and hands rolled him over on his back, Jason's face swinging into view. Doug tried to say something, but nothing came out. Hearing Cat shouting his name, he rolled onto his side.

"Stay down, Dog!" Jason shouted at him over the crowd noise. "The paramedics are on the way. You've gone as far as you can go."

"No!" Doug pushed Jason's hands back. "Not . . . done."

"It's over," Jason snapped back.

Tears streaming down his face, Doug looked into the face of his friend, the young man his sister loved.

"Help . . . me," he begged.

Jason froze for an instant, overcome by the raw misery he'd seen in Doug's eyes. He glanced up at Cat who'd managed to wheel her chair back around to them. She looked at him, too.

"Help us," she asked him.

"Oh, man," Jason muttered. "You guys are *nuts!*" Then he slid his arm around Doug's waist, and Doug seized Jason's shoulder as his friend heaved him up onto his feet. Doug's legs threatened to collapse again, but Jason was there to steady him. Then Doug gripped the left side of the push bar, Jason the right, and with careful precision, they staggered onto the track and the last hundred yards. The people on the sidelines were screaming when they crossed the line.

23
Down Time

The early autumn sun shone warm on his upturned face as Doug sat in the backyard, his left leg propped up by a pillow on the garden bench where he rested. He and Cat and Jason sat together, Cat in her regular wheelchair, Jason cross-legged on the ground, listening to the radio in the background and sipping lemonade.

"So what did the X-rays show?" Jason asked.

"Nothing broken," Doug answered. "It's just a bad sprain."

Cat wheeled over, checked the ice pack, and decided it was still sufficiently cool.

"Gotta keep it elevated, use ice packs, and stay off it for a few more days. I can go back to work on Monday, light duty, and see how it goes."

"Lucky."

Doug nodded.

Their father was off to work, riding high in the opinions of the corporate office who had gotten word about all the free publicity they'd scored because of the race. They regarded Carter Walker with more appreciation than usual.

"Which will last until I do something they don't like," Mr. Carter had said. "'Corp rats' have very short attention spans."

Mother had taken advantage of their notoriety and gone to the insurance company to "light a fire under them" as well.

"If you don't keep after them, they just wander off," she said with a smile.

That left the three of them alone to enjoy the quiet finally. The last couple days had been chaotic.

"The director of the hospital called me yesterday," Jason mentioned. "Apparently you weren't answering the phone for a while."

Doug tried to look innocent, but it was not his best skill.

"Because Cat was so successful as a fund-raiser this year,

they'd like her to consult with the hospital committee that does this year-round. And before you ask, no, it doesn't pay a dime. You'd be the second token member. The first being me."

"I'd have to think about it," Cat said. "I'm busy this fall."

She was back in school part-time. Her independent work had kept her from getting left back, and she was eager to move on into her junior year.

"Speaking of which, your mom says you might be willing to help me with math class," Jason said, putting his hand on hers.

"We can probably arrange something," she answered, squeezing his hand.

"What else is happening?" Jason asked.

For a couple days reporters and photographers from the Bellingham *Herald* and KVOS-TV, the Lynden *Tribune,* and even the Seattle *Post-Intelligencer,* KOMO, and KING-TV had hounded them. In addition, they had done live interviews with various radio stations. But Jason knew about those.

"Well, Jean called this morning."

"Cat's occupational therapist?"

"Uh-huh. Her husband wants to talk to us, maybe write a book about Cat, in light of his wife's therapy and the marathon."

"A book?"

"Just talking," Cat shrugged. "He's a writer, I guess. Thinks there might be a story in it."

"And?" Jason prompted, looking at Doug.

"And what?" Doug replied.

When Cat whacked him on the arm, he grinned.

"And Kristen's coming to dinner tonight to meet the folks."

"Well, well," Jason chuckled. "Good news all around for a change. So . . . what do we do next year?"

"H'mmm?" Cat and Doug said together.

"Going to have to work hard to beat this year." Jason shook his head. "But I have an idea."

Doug felt the laughter welling up inside his heart, and if somebody had asked him right then how he felt, he would have had to say that he felt fine.